Anonymous

The Georgian Bay Canal

SALZWASSER
VERLAG

Anonymous

The Georgian Bay Canal

Reprint of the original.

1st Edition 2023 | ISBN: 978-3-37514-634-4

Verlag (Publisher): Salzwasser Verlag GmbH, Zeilweg 44, 60439 Frankfurt, Deutschland
Vertretungsberechtigt (Authorized to represent): E. Roepke, Zeilweg 44, 60439 Frankfurt, Deutschland
Druck (Print): Books on Demand GmbH, In de Tarpen 42, 22848 Norderstedt, Deutschland

THE

GEORGIAN BAY CANAL.

REPORTS

OF

COL. R. B. MASON, CONSULTING ENGINEER,

AND

KIVAS TULLY, CHIEF ENGINEER;

WITH AN

APPENDIX, PROFILE, AND MAP.

CHICAGO:
DAILY PRESS BOOK AND JOB PRINT, 43 CLARK STREET.

1858.

REPORT.

To George Steel, Thomas Richmond, *and* William Bross, *Committee of Toronto Convention, held Sept. 13th, 1855:*

Gentlemen—In compliance with your request, I visited Canada in the fall of 1855, and examined the proposed route of the Toronto and Georgian Bay Canal, in company with Kivas Tully, Esq., of Toronto, who had then just commenced its survey.

In the examinations made at that time, several routes presented apparent facilities for construction nearly equal, and in view of the great importance of the project, it was deemed essential to make a more extended survey of the country than was at first contemplated.

Mr. Tully has since devoted much time in a careful and thorough examination of four different routes, and the results he presents in his able report, published herewith.

Mr. Tully has so fully discussed all the points relative to the construction of the canal, that I beg to refer to his report for information on that head.

I propose to present in this report,

First —The distance by lake, canal and river, between Chicago and New York, and Chicago and Quebec, by each existing and contemplated route.

Second—Cost of transportation by each route, in vessels of different sizes.

Third—Cost of the canal, tonnage and revenue, with the prospective increase from year to year.

Fourth—Extent of country tributary to the canal, climate, agriculture and mineral resources, extent of country now under cultivation, present population, railway progress, etc.

Fifth —Conclusion.

1st. *The Distance by Lake, Canal and River.*—The following table of distances has been made up from the most reliable information I could obtain by the examination of charts, and by consulting navigators now resident in Chicago. It will be found to vary from the table prepared by Mr. Tully, or from estimates heretofore made. The variation is mainly between Chicago and Buffalo, which has heretofore been computed at 1,100 miles. This distance, no doubt, has been made up from the coasting distances, which has been the route taken generally by vessels heretofore.

But it is believed that a vessel starting from Chicago, and taking the most direct route through the lake, would not necessarily have to go more than 916 miles to reach Buffalo.

Wherever the St. Lawrence river forms a portion of the route, it has been included under the head of lake, as being a navigation not materially more expensive than the lake.

The length of the canals on the routes to New York includes the distance to Albany, and is the actual length in all cases except by the Toronto and Georgian Bay route.

The whole distance in this case from Lake Huron to Lake Ontario, 100 miles, is called canal, whereas 23 miles of it is through Lake Simcoe, and from 15 to 20 miles is what might be termed slack water navigation, having a large extra width, really reducing the distance of actual canal to about 60 miles.

This explanation is due to the Toronto and Georgian Bay route, although in making up the cost of transportation it was deemed advisable to call the entire length a canal.

Comparative Distances of the existing and proposed Routes from Chicago to New York.

ROUTE.	Lake.	Canal.	River.	Total.
Chicago *via* Buffalo to New York...............	916	364	145	1425
" " Welland Canal and Oswego to N. York	1043	237	145	1425
" " Georgian Bay Canal and Oswego to New York..	685	309	145	1138
" " Welland Canal and Lake Champlain to New York.....................	1369	167	145	1681
" " Georgian Bay Canal and Lake Champlain to New York.............	1011	239	145	1395
" " Ottawa Canal and Lake Champlain to New York.....................	896	315	145	1356

Comparative Distances of the existing and proposed Routes from Chicago to Quebec.

ROUTE.	Lake.	Canal.	River.	Total.
Chicago *via* Welland Canal and St. Lawrence to Quebec..........................	1401	69		1470
" " Georgian Bay Canal and St. Lawrence to Quebec.....................	1043	141		1184
" " Ottawa Canal and St. Lawrence to Quebec........................	976	200		1176

2d. *Cost of Transportation.*—In making up these tables it has been assumed that there would be no transhipment at Buffalo and Oswego, but that the Erie and Oswego Canals would be enlarged to the dimensions now proposed for the Erie Canal, and that on all the other routes such improvements would be made as to enable the same vessel loading at Chicago to deliver her cargo in New York or Quebec; and on the route where no transhipment occurs, the price by river is computed the same as by lake.

This difference in the cost of transportation in small and large vessels is only intended to be approximate, the actual result would no doubt be still more favorable for the large vessel.

FROM CHICAGO TO NEW YORK.

ROUTE.	Lake in miles.	Canal in miles.	River in miles.	RATE IN MILLS PER MILE.			Transhipment and port ch'gs.	Total.
				Lake.	Canal.	River.		
300 ton vessel, Buffalo & Erie Canal	916	364	145	3	8	5	10	$6.49
450 " " " " " "	916	364	145	2¾	8	5	10	6.36
600 " " " " " "	916	364	145	2½	8	5	10	6.03
750 " " " " " "	916	364	145	2¼	8	5	10	5.80
1000 " " " " " "	916	364	145	2	8	5	10	5.57
300 ton ves. Welland Canal & Oswego	1043	237	145	3	8	5	10	5.86
450 " " " " " "	1043	237	145	2¾	8	5	10	5.60
600 " " " " " "	1043	237	145	2½	8	5	10	5.34
750 " " " " " "	1043	237	145	2¼	8	5	10	5.08
1000 " " " " " "	1043	237	145	2	8	5	10	4.82
300 ton ves. Geo'n Bay Can. & Oswego	685	309	145	3	8	5	10	5.36
450 " " " " " "	685	309	145	2¾	8	5	10	5.18
600 " " " " " "	685	309	145	2½	8	5	10	5.01
750 " " " " " "	685	309	145	2¼	8	5	10	4.84
1000 " " " " " "	685	309	145	2	8	5	10	4.67

FROM CHICAGO TO NEW YORK.

ROUTE.	Lake in miles.	Canal in miles.	River in miles.	RATE IN MILLS PER MILE.			Total.
				Lake.	Canal.	River.	
300 ton vessels Welland Canal and Lake Champlain............	1369	167	145	3	8	3	$5 89
450 " " "	1369	167	145	2¾	8	2¾	5 50
600 " " "	1369	167	145	2½	8	2½	5 16
750 " " "	1369	167	145	2¼	8	2¼	4 83
1000 " " "	1369	167	145	2	8	2	4 48
300 ton vessel Georgian Bay Canal and Lake Champlain.......	1011	239	145	3	8	3	5 38
450 " " "	1011	239	145	2¾	8	2¾	5 09
600 " " "	1011	239	145	2½	8	2½	4 80
750 " " "	1011	239	145	2¼	8	2¼	4 52
1000 " " "	1011	239	145	2	8	2	4 22
300 ton vessels Ottawa Canal and Lake Champlain............	896	315	145	3	8	3	5 64
450 " " "	896	315	145	2¾	8	2¾	5 38
600 " " "	896	315	145	2½	8	2½	5 12
750 " " "	896	315	145	2¼	8	2¼	4 86
1000 " " "	896	315	145	2	8	2	4 60

CHICAGO TO QUEBEC.

ROUTE.	Lake in miles.	Canal in miles.	River in miles.	RATE IN MILLS PER MILE.			Total.
				Lake.	Canal.	River.	
300 ton vessels by Welland Canal,	1401	69	....	3	8	....	$4 75
450 " " "	1401	69	....	2¾	8	....	4 40
600 " " "	1401	69	....	2½	8	....	4 06
760 " " "	1401	69	....	2¼	8	....	3 70
1000 " " "	1401	69	....	2	8	....	3 35
300 ton vessels by Geo'n Bay Canal	1043	141	....	3	8	....	4 26
450 " " "	1043	141	....	2¾	8	....	4 00
600 " " "	1043	141	....	2½	8	....	3 74
750 " " "	1043	141	....	2¼	8	....	3 48
1000 " " "	1043	141	....	2	8	....	3 22
300 ton vessels by Ottawa Canal..	976	200	....	3	8	....	4 53
450 " " "	976	200	....	2¾	8	....	4 28
600 " " "	976	200	....	2½	8	....	4 04
750 " " "	976	200	....	2¼	8	....	3 80
1000 " " "	976	200	....	2	8	....	3 55

CHICAGO TO LIVERPOOL,
In 1000 Ton Vessels.

Chicago *via* Buffalo to New York............................	$5 57	
New York to Liverpool, 2980 miles at 1½ mills.................	4 47	
		$10 04
Chicago *via* Welland Canal and Oswego to New York...........	$4 82	
To Liverpool	4 47	
		9 29
Chicago *via* Georgian Bay Canal and Oswego to New York	$4 67	
To Liverpool	4 47	
		9 14
Chicago *via* Welland Canal and Lake Champlain to New York.....	$4 48	
To Liverpool	4 47	
		8 95
Chicago *via* Georgian Bay Canal and Lake Champlain to New York,	$4 22	
To Liverpool	4 47	
		8 69
Chicago *via* Ottawa Canal to New York........................	$4 60	
To Liverpool	4 47	
		9 07
Chicago *via* Welland Canal to Quebec.........................	$3 35	
To Liverpool, 2502 miles at 1½ mills..........................	3 75	
		7 10
Chicago *via* Georgian Bay Canal to Quebec	$3 22	
To Liverpool	3 75	
		6 97
Chicago *via* Ottawa Canal to Quebec..........................	$3 55	
To Liverpool	3 75	
		7 30

3d. Cost of the Canal, Tonnage and Revenue. — Of all the routes surveyed by Mr. Tully, Route No. 1, presents the most favorable features and is the one that is recommended. This route commences at the mouth of the Humbee river and passes through Lake Simcoe, terminating at the mouth of the Nottawasago river on Lake Huron. I entirely concur with Mr. Tully in his views of these terminal points. By reference to the profile, it will be seen that the ascent from Lake Ontario to the summit is quite uniform and gradual, admitting of a series of combined locks as shown on the profile, or in some cases of single locks with sufficient space between them for passing vessels.

The combined plan gives larger reaches between the locks and has some advantages in that respect for towing vessels. But these advantages are more than counterbalanced by the delay that must necessarily occur by such an arrangement of locks unless they are double locks, particularly when the canal is worked up to near its full capacity.

Wherever it was practicable, therefore, I should advise the single lock, with sufficient space between for the convenient passing of vessels, or, when combined, that they should be constructed with a view to adding a double lock at a future day. No work of a difficult character presents itself until we reach the summit level; there we encounter a cut of nearly 200 feet at the deepest point, averaging about 90 feet for nearly ten miles. This is probably a larger and more extensive cut than has ever before been encountered on any public work, but the examinations, so far as made, do not show any thing insurmountable in its execution. Such allowance has been made in the estimate for contingencies as seemed necessary from all the information that has been obtained. It would be desirable, however, as this is the only serious obstacle, to have a more thorough examination made at this point with a view to ascertain with more certainty the quality of material to be encountered in making the cut.

The navigation through Lake Simcoe is favorable, with a sufficient depth of water for safety.

The cut between Lake Simcoe and the Nottawasago river averages about 50 feet for several miles, but there is nothing that indicates anything unfavorable or very formidable. From its entrance into the Nottawasago Valley to the western terminal point it is exceedingly favorable, except a short cut near the lake. The most part of this distance would be a very considerable extra width of water surface, affording a fine navigation. The Nottawasago river for some four miles from its entrance into the lake runs nearly parallel with the lake and is from 300 to 600 feet wide, with an averge depth from 10 to 12 feet water, and at a very small expense may be made a perfectly safe harbor for a very large number of vessels.

Mr Tully's estimate for the route described is.................$22,170,750

Six per cent. interest on this sum would be per year............ 1,330,245
For repairs and maintainance of the canal, say $1000 per mile or
    per year..   100,000
                                                         _____
                                                          $1,430,245

In order to pay 6 per cent. on its cost and maintain it, we require an income of $1,430,245; will the country tributary to it afford a business that will justify this expense for its accommodation? By refering to what has been done in times past we may draw conclusions for the future.

In Messrs. Parkinson and Smith's report on the St. Clair, Chatham and Rond Eau Ship Canal, they estimate the total tonnage passing St. Clair flats in 1855, between the ports of Chicago, Milwaukee, Toledo, Cleveland, Buffalo, Oswego, and Ogdensburg, at 2,385,516 tons. Taking into account the smaller ports on the lake it will be safe to call the tonnage in 1855, 2,500,000. I am confirmed in my opinion that this amount is not over estimated, by consulting the very able report of Col. J. D. Graham, U. S. Army, on the commerce of the lakes, and various other authorities.

In the very valuable reports of John B. Jarvis, Esq., on the Caughnawaga Canal, and of William J. McAlpine, Esq., in 1853, then State Engineers of New York, I find that Mr. Jarvis estimates that the tonnage from 1853 would be doubled in six years and quadrupled in fifteen years, and that the total movement to and from tide water in 1868, from and to points west of Buffalo would be 9,000,000 tons. Mr. McAlpine estimates the movement on the Erie Canal in 1852 at a little more than 3,000,000 tons; allowing the same rate of increase as estimated by Mr. Jarvis would very soon work the canal up to its full capacity in its enlarged state.

Assuming then the tonnage that passed the St. Clair flats in 1855 to have been 2,500,000, and allowing one third of this amount for the business between the ports and Lake Erie and points north and west of the St. Clair flats, we have left 1,666,667 tons as the amount that would probably have passed through the Georgian Bay Canal had it been completed in 1855. I assume as the rate of increase 29 per cent. for every five years. The reasons for this are particularly set forth in another part of this report. And assuming the tolls on the canal to be four mills per ton per mile, or forty cents per ton, we have the following result:

Year.	Total Tonnage.	The portion of Tonnage that would pass the Canal.	Tolls.
1855	2,500,000	1,666,667	
1857	2,790,000	1,860,000	
1860	3,275,460	2,183,640	
1865	4,225,343	2,816,895	1,126,758
1870	5,450,692	3,633,794	1,453,517
1875	7,031,392	4,587,594	1,835,037
1880	9,070,495	5,917,996	2,367,198
1885	11,700,938	7,634,214	3,053,686
1890	15,094,210	9,848,136	3,939,254
1895	19,471,530	12,704,095	5,081,638

This canal, if commenced soon and prosecuted with the energy it should be, may be in successful operation in 1865. We commence then with a business nearly equal to six per cent. on its cost, with a certain prospect of a rapid increase.

The lumber trade I have not considered in my estimate of the tonnage. The letter marked "A," see Appendix, from H. R. A. Boys Esq., of Baine, Canada, will give an idea of what may be expected from that source.

EXTENT OF COUNTRY TRIBUTARY TO THE CANAL.

In this, as in other portions of this report, the reader is requested to place before him any good map of North America. It will be seen that the great central valley of the continent, lying between the Alleghany and the Rocky Mountains, stretches from the Gulf of Mexico to the Arctic Ocean. This magnificent valley—for there is no chain of mountains east and west to divide it—is drained to the south by the Mississippi, to the east, by the St. Lawrence to the Atlantic, and by the Seven, Nelson's, and other rivers, into Hudson's Bay, and to the north by Mackenzie's river, which empties into the Arctic Ocean. The great controlling streams of commerce have always followed the lines of longitude, and it needs no argument to show that the trade of the central portions of this vast valley—the largest and the richest upon the globe—must flow east and west through the lakes and the valley of the St. Lawrence. The north and south traffic upon the Mississippi and its tributaries will ever be large and important, but, as compared with the commerce upon the lakes, and eastward, through the Erie canal and the St. Lawrence, to the ocean, the trade upon the Mississippi must ever fall far below, both in bulk and value, that upon the lakes and the St. Lawrence.

It will be conceded at once that the Georgian Bay Canal will be a competitor for the trade with the seaboard of all the country east of the Rocky Mountains, and west and north-west of the southern point of Lake Michigan. By the Illinois Central Railroad wheat is brought from the southern counties of that state to the Chicago Market, and it will be certainly safe to say that the lake route will attract the trade as far south as the latitude of Alton. Drawing a line, therefore, east and west through Alton, and extending it to the Rocky Mountains, we shall have within the bounds of the United States, east of the Rocky Mountains and west of Lake Michigan, 700,000 square miles; territory enough to form fourteen states as large as Ohio. There is much more territory than this, but it is intended only to embrace that which is valuable and available for settlement and profitable cultivation. The report of H. U. Hind, Esq., Naturalist and Geologist of the recent Canadian expedition to the Red River of the North, gives the amount of territory available and valuable for settlement, north of the boundary of the United States, and drained by the rivers flowing into Lake Winipeg, at 400,000 square miles. It is safe to say, therefore, that the commerce of 1,100,000 square miles of the great central valley of the American continent, would be tributary to the Georgian Bay Canal. It has been stated by men whose judgment is worthy of respect at 2,000,000 of square miles; but we prefer to be far within rather than beyond the true estimate. This vast territory is equal to one-third of the entire area of the United States, and, Russia excepted, is nearly equal to that of all Europe combined.

COMMERCIAL FACILITIES.

To illustrate this topic by particulars would require a much larger space than the limits of this report will permit. The magnificent chain of lakes extending west far away towards the center of the continent, and affording nearly all the advantages of ocean navigation, is a most wonderful provision of Providence to promote the commercial, and hence the social, welfare of the millions who are soon to inhabit this valley. So gentle are its slopes that the large rivers which drain it into the Gulf of Mexico and Hudson's Bay, the Mississippi and its tributaries, and the rivers flowing into and draining Lake Winipeg, are navigable for steamers for thousands of miles. No country in the world presents a finer field for railway enterprise, and as it fills up with a vigorous, industrious, intelligent population, these advantages will be fully appreciated and improved.

CLIMATE.

The climate of that portion of the territory in the United States that would be tributary to the Georgian Bay Canal, belongs to the most healthy and inviting portions of the temperate zone. It is the range which, in all ages of the past, has nourished the most populous and powerful empires, and that such is the "manifest destiny" of the country under consideration all who have studied its character and resources have entire confidence. Of the 400,000 miles of territory in the valleys of the Red River of the North, the Assinniboin, the Saskatchewan, and surrounding Lake Winipeg, recent investigations have shown that its climate is well adapted to promote the health and the vigorous development of the human family. Mr. Hind, whose report is referred to above, says that "all the necessaries of life are found in the Red river valley. All crops cultivated in Canada succeed well, and often show an average yield far in excess of Canadian returns. The climate of the agricultural season is well adapted to all the operations of husbandry. Corresponding observations show that the summer temperature is three or four degrees warmer than at Toronto." The winter climate, he adds, "is very severe." Though severe, all experience has proved that the winter is bracing, and not unfavorable to the ordinary out-door operations of this season in northern latitudes. The recent large and elaborate work of Prof. Blodgett on climatology has proved that the climactic lines, when they pass west of Lake Superior, bend far away to the north; and this eminent climatologist gives it as his well matured opinion that the climate of the region under consideration is highly favorable to the development of a great, prosperous and powerful people.

AGRICULTURAL RESOURCES.

In agricultural resources it is conceded by all who understand the subject that no portion of the globe, of equal extent, contains so rich a soil, or so many elements of all that can contribute to the physical comfort and the social elevation of man. All the cereals are produced in great abundance; fruits of all kinds common in corresponding latitudes are matured in the greatest perfection; and horses, mules, cattle, sheep, swine, poultry, and all the domestic animals, are produced in the greatest abundance. If fully developed, there can be no question whatever that the soil of this vast region would support a population as dense as that of any other portion of the globe, and afford the means for the highest physical, intellectual and social development. Should we speak by particulars, and give figures and estimates, from well-known facts, as to its productive capacity, they would appear more like the extravagant musings of a vagrant imagination than the deductions of sober matter-of-fact reality.

MINERAL RESOURCES.

COPPER. — Both in extent and richness the copper mines of Lake Superior are without a rival. The actual figures showing the size of masses of native copper found in the Minnesota, the Cliff, and some of the other mines appear absolutely fabulous. There are hundreds of square miles on the south shore of Lake Superior whose strata are filled with copper, and an abundance of this metal is found there to supply the world for ages to come.

IRON. — The reputation of the Lake Superior iron as among the very best in the world is now generally established. Mountains of this essential element of civilization exist there, sufficient alone to supply the entire continent for an indefinite period in the future. It is also found in Illinois, Wisconsin, Iowa and Minnesota, in some districts in great abundance. Facts are not wanting to prove its existence in that part of the British possessions under consideration, and in some portions it is believed that it will be found in large quantities.

COAL. — Illinois contains one of the largest and ere long it must become one of the most productive coal fields in the world. It also extends into Iowa and exists there in large quantities. In relation to the northern portion of the territory under consideration in the United States, and that which is embraced in the

British possessions, the following facts are quoted from an able and most valuable lecture on "The Undeveloped Northern Portion of the American Continent," delivered before Bell's Commercial College, Chicago, February, 1856, by JOHN L. SCRIPPS, Esq., editor of the CHICAGO DAILY PRESS. The lecturer (page 17) says:

"I remark in the next place upon the existence of coal in a large portion of the country. Franchere and Gov. Simpson speak of its outcropping at different places on the Saskatchewan. Lewis and Clark saw bituminous coal between Fort Clark and the falls of the Missouri River. Culbertson also saw coal in the same localities. Wyeth saw large quantities of it on the Yellowstone. Gov. Stevens' party found the whole country from the falls of the Missouri westward to the mountains, nearly five hundred miles, underlaid with lignite. Bonneville speaks of regions among the mountains near the head waters of the Yellowstone, which abound in anthracite coal. In fact, coal has been traced along the 47th parallel of latitude for a distance of nearly ten degrees of longitude, with a southern outcrop, rendering it more than probable, when considered in connection with the discoveries of coal in the Saskatchewan, the Alhabasca, Mackenzie's River, and Great Bear Lake, that a coal field of greater extent than any other in the world exists in the western half of the district of country included in our subject. Further evidence is found to support this hypothesis in the discoveries of coal nearly all around the northern rim of the North American continent by the captains of whaling vessels, and by the hardy explorers who have tempted the Artic seas in search of a north-west passage, by the presence of both coal and lignite in Greenland, upon Disco Island and upon the Faroe Islands, off the coast of Greenland—thus indicating the wonderful economy of nature, or rather the existence a beneficent Providential design, by which regions destitute of timber are supplied with an easily accessible fuel."

LEAD. — The extent and the resources of the Galena lead district are already very generally known. As in the magnitude of her lakes and rivers, so in the bestowment of her mineral treasures in this vast country, Nature has distributed with a most bountiful hand. There is here enough and to spare of this valuable mineral, for all the people that can ever find a home upon the American continent.

In summing up the mineral resources of the northern portion of the American continent, Mr. Scripps, in his lecture above quoted, says:

"The most extensive systems of salt springs and lakes abound in this region, in different localities, both within the American and the British Possessions, and in some districts the mineral itself is found in great purity and abundance.

"Considering the vast amount of minerals already discovered with scarcely any scientific exploration, the hypothesis is by no means an unreasonable one, that no portion of the continent exceeds this vast undeveloped north-west in mineral resources."

EXTENT OF TERRITORY NOW UNDER CULTIVATION.

It is impossible to estimate with any certain approach to accuracy, the amount of this vast region that is now actually under cultivation. The rapidity of the growth of the North-west has so far exceeded all former ratios of increase that one scarcely dares to believe the figures when the census returns show the acknowledged results from one decade to another. In 1850 the amount of land in that portion of the United States now under consideration which was then under cultivation, as shown by the census returns, was as follows:

Illinois,	5,039,545
Wisconsin,	1,045,499
Iowa,	824,682
Minnesota,	5,035
Total,	6,914,761

This is an area of 10,804 square miles, only about one-fifth of the area of the State of Illinois. Since 1850 we have no returns to show the amount of land brought under cultivation, but the statistics of population, as will hereafter appear, show an increase of 65 per cent. in five years, from 1850 to 1855, in the states above named; and the increase for the same period in these states, and Indiana, Ohio and Michigan, show a gain of 29 per cent. With the ratio of 29 per cent., there would be 8,920,041 acres under cultivation in 1855, and at the close of 1857, 9,954,765 acres, equal to 15,554 square miles.

———

PRESENT POPULATION,

And its probable increase, and also that of the lands brought under cultivation, Commerce, etc.

The population of the district in the United States, now under consideration, in 1850, '55, '57, as derived from the government and state census, and other sources, was about as follows:

	1850.	1855.	1857.
Illinois,	851,479	1,300,250	1,500,000
Wisconsin,	305,391	551,109	650,000
Iowa,	192,215	345,985	690,000
Minnesota,	6,077	40,000	200,000
Nebraska,		4,000	30,000
	1,355,162	2,241,344	3,070,000

These figures, as above stated, show an increase from 1850 to 1855, of some 65 per cent.; but if the States of Ohio, Indiana and Michigan be added to the above, as they are commonly included in speaking of the North-west, the ratio is brought down to 29 per cent. which we prefer to take as a basis for future calculations. Taking these figures as the ratio for thirty-seven years, which is a fraction more than the average lifetime of a generation, we present the following table, showing the probable increase of population, and the amount of lands to be brought under cultivation for every five years, from 1855 to 1895.

From the very able and valuable report of Col. J. D. Graham, U. S. Army, on the commerce of the lake ports for 1855, we find that the total value of the commerce of Chicago and Milwaukee which passed over the St. Clair Flats for that year, was $136,304,692.72. Adding only the value of the commerce of Milwaukee for that of all the other ports on lake Michigan, we shall have $159,109,130.55 as the total value of the commerce from lake Michigan which passed over the St. Clair Flats in 1855.

POPULATION, COMMERCE, TONNAGE, ETC.

The following Table shows the Present Population, amount of Land now under Cultivation, Commerce of Lake Michigan which would be tributary to the Georgian Bay Canal, or for which it would be a competitor, Estimated Revenue, with the Tonnage and Cost of Freight, on Vessels which passed over the St. Clair Flats in 1855, with their Probable Increase for thirty-seven years, at the rate of 29 per cent. for every five years—29 per cent. being the Ratio of the Increase from 1850 to 1855, of the Population of the States commonly included in the term North West, viz.: Ohio, Indiana, Illinois, Michigan, Wisconsin, Iowa, and Minnesota.

	1855.	1857.	1860.	1865.	1870.	1875.	1880.	1885.	1890.	1895.
Population,	2,957,844	3,050,000	3,664,170	4,649,382	5,997,713	7,726,652	9,966,795	12,875,925	16,609,944	21,425,666
Total number of acres of land under actual cultivation,	8,929,041	9,951,745	11,666,891	15,076,093	19,445,150	25,068,125	32,362,681	41,749,118	52,656,500	69,474,756
Total of lands cultivated in square miles,	13,937	15,554	18,220	23,556	30,387	39,200	50,568	65,238	84,150	108,554
Amount of land remaining at each period to be cultivated in square miles,	1,056,063	1,054,446	1,051,750	1,046,441	1,049,613	1,031,800	1,019,432	1,004,767	1,015,820	991,466
Value of the commerce of Lake Michigan passing over St. Clair Flats,	$158,169,151	177,565,780	208,462,985	268,916,325	346,902,067	447,503,769	577,179,629	744,690,721	960,651,030	1,239,239,425
Tonnage passing St. Clair Flats in 1854, with its prospective increase,	2,400,000	2,700,000	3,275,400	4,225,266	5,450,592	7,061,292	9,679,452	11,700,925	15,094,192	19,471,307
Estimated amount of Tonnage that would pass through the canal,	1,666,667	1,866,000	2,182,640	2,816,885	3,633,781	4,587,361	5,917,396	7,631,242	9,848,346	12,704,965
Estimated revenue for the canal,				1,126,753	1,453,515	1,835,867	2,367,494	3,053,686	3,929,554	5,081,636

Let us discuss the facts contained in this table for a few moments; and first, as to population. It may be said that the ration of twenty-nine per cent. will not be continued through thirty-seven years. As above stated, the ratio of the increase of population in the territory west of Lake Michigan, for the last five years, has been sixty-five per cent.—more than twice the figures from which our results are derived.

Take another fact. The census returns show that the entire North-west, embracing Ohio, Indiana, Illinois, Wisconsin, with the addition, now, of Iowa, Minnesota and Nebraska, in 1820, contained 792,719 inhabitants; in 1857—the same period on which our results are based—they contained, in round numbers, 7,200,000 people, an increase in a little more than the average life time of one generation of EIGHT HUNDRED PER CENT. With railways and telegraphs, and magnificent steamers on lake and river, and withal, the knowledge of the agricultural and mineral wealth of this vast country, the beauty and magnitude of its prairies, and the salubrity of its climate, now matters of daily conversation and newspaper comment in every portion of the civilized world, who shall say that the increase of population in this broad, favored land will not equal, in the next thirty-seven years, the results of the same period in the past. Leaving out Ohio, Michigan and Indiana, that ratio would give, west of Lake Michigan, in 1895, within the territory of the United States, north of the latitude of Alton and east of the Rocky Mountains, a population of 24,560,000. This result is truly amazing ; but it is not more wonderful than what a large proportion of those now living, both in the United States and in Canada, have themselves seen and realized. Take still another illustration. The old northern States proper have increased in the last thirty-seven years in the ratio of eighty-five per cent. It has been proved from the statistics of our railways for the past few years, and other sources, that about 250,000 people have annually emigrated into the country west of Lake Michigan. Apply the ratio of the increase of population of the old States to those already in the territory under consideration, and half the ratio for half the time, to this stream of human energy that is constantly flowing into it, and we still have, in 1895, a population of 19,787,000. It is therefore deemed a moderate estimate to say that the portion of territory in the United States that is tributary to the Georgian Bay Canal will contain, only thirty-seven years hence, a population of at least TWENTY MILLIONS OF SOULS.

The question next in order is, what will be the population of the territory under consideration that is within the British possessions? There are no facts within our reach to show what the present population of the valley of the Red River of the North, and at the trading posts of the Hudson's Bay Company, is; but several thousands, it is believed, are already there. Any calculations, however, based upon their probable increase, would fall far within the mark. For scores of years the Hudson Bay Company have kept the world in ignorance as to the extent and the richness of the country lying north and west of Lake Superior, using all the means in their power to strengthen the conviction that it was a cold, inhospitable region, fit only for the residence of Indians and trappers, and the wild animals whose furs were the only productions of this vast territory that could be made available for civilized man. The gigantic monopoly of this company is now, or soon will be, broken; the ignorance which it so industriously fostered, is now dissipated, and the people of Canada and Great Britain will assert their right to emigrate to and settle in this vast, rich, and inviting region. An immense stream of active, intelligent and enterprising men will, ere the next decade shall have passed away, be pouring into it from Canada, England, Ireland and Scotland, and by the year 1895, the foundations of a great and prosperous empire will be laid there, numbering even then, at a moderate estimate, from one to two millions of people. It may be asked in general, and it is certainly a pertinent question, where all these people to settle that portion of the United States and the British possessions are to come from? We answer: They will be the intelligent, the enterprising, and the vigorous sons and daughters of Canada and the older states of the American Union. Immense navies will be put in commission to transport to this favored land the same class of emigrants from England, Ireland, Scotland, France, Holland, Germany, and nearly all the other kingdoms and empires of Europe. Where land is cheap, the soil rich and productive, the climate inviting, and withal, the government free and stable, and life and property secure, there will the intelligent millions of our race congregate for the next half century.

Let us canvass next the amount of land likely to be brought under cultivation. It may have been noticed in this, as in regard to population, that the whole of Illinois is included in our calculations; but about half the state of Missouri lies north of the latitude of Alton, and having no means to divide either state, if the southern section of the one be taken for the northern section of the other, the results will be sufficiently accurate for all practical purposes. The amount of territory likely to be under cultivation in the different periods, as stated in the table, is far too low. It is much too small now. The population of the territory under consideration increased, from 1850 to 1855, in the ratio of sixty-five per cent., instead of twenty-nine, the element used in the preparation of the table. There can scarcely be a doubt that there was twice as much land under cultivation in 1857 in Illinois, Wisconsin, Iowa and Minnesota, as there was in 1850. We shall be disappointed if the census returns of 1860 do not show an increase of three hundred per cent. since 1850. At that time there were 6,914,761 acres under actual cultivation, as shown by the United States census. An increase of three hundred per cent. would give, in 1860, 20,744,283 acres, or 32,413 square miles, and not 18,260 as shown in the table.

We must wait for the result of the census of 1860, to learn the actual amount of land which the hardy sons of the west shall have brought under cultivation, but the figures which exhibit the commerce of the lakes, as shown by Col. Graham's report above referred to, and the statistics of the commerce of Chicago for the past few years as proved by the able and carefully prepared statistical articles of the Chicago DAILY PRESS, afford one of the most important subjects of study to be found in the annals of modern commercial progress. Thirty years ago the commerce of Lake Michigan was merely nominal, confined to an occasional visit of a small government vessel with supplies to the forts in the adjoining territories. In 1855, its value, as deduced from Col. Graham's report, was $159,109,131. To be more particular, we present the following table, showing the receipts and shipments of grain at the port of Chicago for the last four years:

TOTAL RECEIPTS.

	1854.	1855.	1856.	1857.
Wheat, bush	3,038,955	7,535,097	8,767,760	10,554,761
Corn	7,490,753	8,532,377	11,888,398	7,409,130
Oats	4,194,385	2,947,188	2,219,897	1,707,245
Rye	85,691	68,086	45,707	87,911
Barley	201,764	201,895	128,457	127,689
Total	15,011,548	19,284,643	23,050,219	19,886,756
Flour into wheat	792,875	1,203,310	1,624,605	1,969,670
Total	15,804,423	20,487,953	24,674,824	21,856,406

Total Shipments.

	1854.	1855.	1856.	1857.
Wheat, bush......	2,206,725	6,288,155	8,337,420	9,185,052
Corn............	6,837,890	7,517,625	11,129,668	6,814,615
Oats	3,229,987	1,899,538	1,014,548	416,778
Rye	41,157	19,318	599	....
Barley	148,421	92,082	19,051	17,993
Total	12,364,185	15,816,718	20,501,276	16,734,438
Flour into Wheat..	538,135	817,095	1,081,945	1,298,240
Total	12,902,320	16,633,813	21,583,221	18,032,678

The following table of the receipts of lumber, shows the steady and wonderful growth of that trade for the last eleven years :

	Lumber, ft.	Shingles.	Lath.
1847................	32,118,325	12,148,500	5,655,700
1848................	60,009,250	20,000,000	10,025,109
1849................	73,259,553	39,057,750	19,281,753
1850................	100,364,779	55,423,750	19,809,700
1851................	125,056,437	60,338,250	27,583,175
1852................	147,816,232	77,080,500	19,759,670
1853................	202,101,098	93,483,784	39,133,116
1854................	228,336,783	28,061,250	32,431,550
1855................	306,553,467	158,770,860	46,487,550
1856................	556,673,169	135,876,000	79,235,120
1857................	459,639,198	131,852,250	80,130,000

The following table shows the number of arrivals at the port of Chicago in 1857, with the tonnage and number of men :

Number and Tonnage of vessels arrived at the Port of Chicago for the Season of 1857.

	Stmrs.	Props.	Sail.	Total.	Tonnage.	Men.
March	..	3	16	19	3,236	124
April	30	28	248	306	16,813	4,795
May	50	56	800	906	208,500	8,869
June...........	49	92	900	1,041	218,108	8,932
July	41	96	923	1,060	223,700	8,899
August..........	46	96	917	1,059	273,105	10,136
September.......	42	109	735	886	227,785	8,737
October	34	91	589	714	263,672	7,287
November	12	41	269	322	74,485	3,225
December	2	6	36	44	11,209	454
Total	306	618	5,433	6,357	1,460,613	61,458
Arrivals unreported, (estimated)..........				1,200	292,800	7,200
Total				7,557	1,753,413	68,658
Total in 1856.............				7,328	1,515,379	65,552
Total in 1855.............				6,610	1,608,845	
Total in 1854.............				5,021	1,092,644	

There were laid up in winter quarters at this port, 1857–8, 7 steamers, 29 propellers and 214 sail vessels.

POPULATION OF CHICAGO.

We present the following table showing the population of Chicago at different periods:

1840	4,470	1850	28,269
1843	7,580	1852	38,733
1845	12,088	1853	60,652
1846	14,169	1854	65,872
1847	16,859	1855	83,509
1848	20,035	1856	110,000
1849	23,047	1857	130,000

RAILWAY PROGRESS.

In January 1852, there was but one railway, the Galena, forty miles long, entering Chicago. The list of roads whose business tends to swell the commerce of that city, now actually completed and in operation, is as follows:

	Miles.
Chicago and Milwaukee	85
Kenosha and Rockford	11
Racine and Mississippi	86
Chicago, St. Paul and Fond du Lac	131
Milwaukee and Mississippi (Western Division)	130
Galena and Chicago Union	121
Fox River Valley	34
Wisconsin Central	8
Beloit Branch	20
Beloit and Madison	17
Mineral Point	32
Dubuque and Pacific	29
Galena (Fulton) Air Line	136
Chicago, Iowa and Nebraska	36
Chicago, Burlington and Quincy	210
Burlington and Missouri	35
Quincy and Chicago	100
Hannibal and St. Joseph	65
Chicago and Rock Island	182
Mississippi and Missouri, 1st Division	55
" " 2d "	20
" " 3d "	13
Peoria and Bureau Valley	47
Peoria and Oquawka	143
St. Louis, Alton and Chicago	284
Illinois Central	704
Pittsburgh, Fort Wayne and Chicago	383
Michigan Southern and Northern Indiana	242
Cincinnati, Peru and Chicago	28
Michigan Central	282
New Albany and Salem	284

Eleven trunk and twenty branch and extension lines............ 3,953

The total earnings of all these roads for 1856, were $17,343,242.83, in 1857 they were $18,590,520.26. Only six years previous, the earnings of the forty miles in operation, were a mere nominal sum. The State of Illinois alone has now 2,775 miles of completed railway; six years ago it had but 95. Comment upon the above tables and figures, for which we are indebted to the valuable yearly statistical articles of the Chicago DAILY PRESS, is entirely unnecessary; they show more clearly than language possibly can, the rapid progress of the North-West in wealth, population and the means of commercial and social intercourse. Let it be observed that the commerce with the seaboard of all the country bordering upon the railways centering in Chicago, with the exception of the three eastern lines, the Michigan Central, the Michigan Southern and the Pittsburgh roads, would be tributary to the Georgian Bay Canal. But this is not all. By the time the canal can be completed, thousands of miles more of railway, extending in every direction through this vast, fertile region, will be pouring the wealth of millions of enterprising, energetic freemen into the navies of Lake Michigan, and the great majority of that commerce will flow through this magnificent highway, for the trade of the continent and the St. Lawrence to the ocean. An empire will by that time have grown up north and west of Lake Superior, which will contribute its traffic to swell the receipts and reward the enterprise of those who shall build this canal.

CONCLUSION.

By reference to the preceding tables it will be seen that the Georgian Bay route is nearly three hundred miles shorter than any other except the Ottawa route, that it is 90 cents per ton cheaper than *via* Buffalo, and 15 cents per ton cheaper than *via* Welland Canal and Oswego. That by the Lake Champlain route, the Georgian Bay route is 26 cents per ton cheaper than *via* Welland Canal, and 38 cents per ton cheaper than *via* the Ottawa route.

That to Quebec the Georgian Bay route is 13 cents per ton cheaper than *via* Welland Canal, and 33 cents per ton cheaper than *via* the Ottawa route.

In point of time the Georgian Bay route would save about one day over any other. In comparing the Georgian Bay route *via* Oswego, Champlain and Montreal, we find that the route *via*

Champlain is 45 cents per ton cheaper than via Oswego, and to Quebec is $1.45 per ton cheaper than via Oswego, and $1.00 per ton cheaper than via Champlain. There can hardly be a doubt but what this margin is sufficient to secure at least a fair proportion of the immense trade of the west through the St. Lawrence, and I can see no good reason why it should not secure much the largest share of it.

On the Ottawa route, not having very reliable information about it, but knowing that over 400 miles of it would be close navigation, I have assumed 200 of it to be canal, or equal to a canal in expense of navigation. Several objections present themselves to this route:

1st. The route being so much farther north there would be a loss of from two to four weeks time each year in the navigation.

2d. It enters the St. Lawrence at a point where the trade must necessarily go down the St. Lawrence instead of having a choice of routes, unless the Caughnawaga Canal is built, and in that event it would not have the choice *via* Oswego.

3d. The trade would be more divided between that route and Buffalo than it would be between the Georgian Bay route and Buffalo, for much that passes through the Georgian Bay route would be intercepted at Oswego and pass through more than 200 miles of the New York canals.

4th. The entire business would be lost to the St. Lawrence canals, and the direct benefit to Canada would be far less than by the construction of the Georgian Bay canal.

The Georgian Bay route has the advantage of good navigation to and from it, avoiding St. Clair flats and the dangerous navigation of Lake Erie, and at a moderate expense may have safe and commodious harbors at each end of it. There would be a saving of nearly 300 miles in distance, a saving in expense of transportation, and of time and insurance. It enters Lake Ontario at a point where if the Caughnawaga Canal is built, trade has a choice of three routes to tide water, and the entire business from two of them would pass through the St. Lawrence canals. It will be seen by Mr. Tully's report that the supply of water is abundant, not only for the canal but for extensive water power, and that all the materials required in its construction are convenient.

It has been assumed in the comparison of the routes that the St. Clair flats would be improved so as to admit the passage of 1000 ton vessels. How difficult this would be I am unable to say, but I am credibly informed that the expenditures at that point heretofore has not produced any beneficial effects in the improvement of navigation. It is probable, therefore, that in the event of this route being improved, that there would be more liability of interruption and detention than by the Georgian Bay route.

When we take into view the vast extent of country whose business must seek an outlet through this channel, the conviction is irresistible that the wants and necessities of the west will not be met until the Georgian Bay and Caughnawaga Canals are constructed, the Oswego and Champlain canals enlarged—the first equal to the Erie canal and the last for the passage of 1000 ton vessels, and the St. Lawrence improved for the passage of the same sized vessels.

When this is done a direct trade will be opened between Chicago and all parts of the world. To doubt this would be to doubt the intelligence and energy of the business men of Chicago, Milwaukee and the Lake Michigan cities.

They have already in fact, commenced the trade, and nothing is required for its successful prosecution but an improvement of the navigation, so as to admit of a large class of vessels.

Let us examine for a moment the cost of these improvements.

Georgian Bay Canal	$22,170,750
Caughnawaga Canal	4,267,890
Champlain Canal, Estimated	6,000,000
Improvement of the Hudson, say	2,000,000
St. Lawrence Canal, Estimated	6,000,000
Total	$40,438,640

But suppose they cost $50,000,000, where, I would ask, among the hundreds of millions of dollars that have been spent in public improvements could you select the expenditure of $50,000,000, the benefits of which are so widely diffused and promising such vast results in the future as would the completion of these improvements under consideration?

Let the cities of Canada awake to their true interest; let them unite heartily in this enterprise, and great as it confessedly is, it can certainly, I might add easily, be accomplished. It would secure beyond a peradventure, for the cities of the St. Lawrence, Toronto, Montreal and Quebec, a leading and a commanding position upon the American continent.

In this connection I quote the language of Wm. Bross, Esq., editor of the Chicago DAILY PRESS, who, from the commencement of this important exterprise, has devoted much time and energy to bring it before the public, used in a speech before the convention at Toronto, Sept. 13th, 1855 :

"I once heard Capt. Hugunin, a veteran sailor of our city, who commenced his eventful career on Lake Ontario, in 1812, after referring to the growth and endless prospective value of the products of the west, say, 'That the great God, when he made the mighty west, made also the lakes and the mighty St. Lawrence to float their commerce to the ocean;' and, I might add, as well attempt to lead the boiling current of Niagara to the sea in hose-pipe, as to ship the products of these 700,000 square miles to the ocean by the Erie and the Welland Canals and all the railways now or hereafter to be constructed."

The same gentleman, in an article in the PRESS, after showing the immense benefits which the Georgian Bay Canal would confer upon Toronto, closes with the following paragraph in relation to Montreal, applicable, with nearly equal force, to Quebec :

"For the purpose of direct trade with Europe, it matters little whether vessels (from the lakes) go directly through, or whether cargoes are transhipped at Montreal. In our judgment, certainly during the summer, transhipment there into very large ocean vessels and steamers would be found the most profitable. In the winter, propellers and sail vessels, especially if they rated at one thousand tons, might find it more profitable to escape from the embargo of ice upon the lakes, and spend the winter in the American or European coasting trade. But in any event, Montreal would hold the key to all the immense trade of the west, flowing down the St. Lawrence to the ocean. Her merchants would furnish assorted cargoes of goods for the west from all parts of the globe, from which full cargoes could not be made up to the lake cities. In any event, she would be to the trade of the St. Lawrence what New York is to that of the Hudson. It needs but the enterprise on the part of her citizens corresponding to the magnitude of the interests at stake, to secure for her this proud position, beyond any contingency. It is true that national pride and immense capital, and the beaten track of commerce, are on the side of New York; but God and nature are stronger than all these, and let any intelligent man compare the "Erie ditch" with the mighty St. Lawrence, with a canal to pass vessels of 1,000 tons burthen from Georgian Bay to Toronto, and he cannot doubt for a moment on which side the immutable laws of commerce will decide the contest.'"

I am much indebted to the valuable reports of Col. J. D. Graham, U. S. Army, John B. Jervis, and William J. McAlpine, Esqrs., and to William Bross, Esq., editor of the Chicago DAILY PRESS, and others, for much important statistical information.

Very respectfully submitted,

R. B. MASON, *Consulting Engineer*

REPORT,

BY KIVAS TULLY, ESQ.

CHIEF ENGINEER'S OFFICE, }
Toronto, January 15th, 1858. }

SIR: On the 14th of September, 1855, the Committee appointed by the convention of delegates from Chicago, Oswego, Toronto and Barrie, instructed me " to complete the survey of a route for the canal from Toronto *via* Lake Simcoe to the Georgian Bay on Lake Huron, and to report to this Committee, with a topographical description of the country, levels, heights, sections, and approximate estimates for the construction of a canal capable of passing vessels of one thousand tons burthen; a profile of the line to be furnished with the report."

The Committee also arranged that the members of the Chicago delegation should secure the services of one of the most eminent engineers, to go over the ground with Mr. Tully, and act with him as consulting engineer in the progress of the survey.

In accordance with the tenor of the above resolutions, I herewith submit my report on the several proposed routes to which I consider my duties to have been confined, leaving to the consulting engineer, Col. R. B. Mason, of Chicago, the important task of furnishing the necessary statistical information in reference to the extent of the anticipated trade that may be relied on as the means of defraying the cost of construction.

In my preliminary report to you as President of the Board of Trade, containing a statement of the field operations of the various routes, dated the 22d of January, 1857, it is mentioned that between the 16th and 23d of November, 1856, I accompanied Col. Mason, the consulting engineer, when he made an examination of the route; and at a conference with the Committee held afterward, a further survey of the route between Lake Couchiching, at the north-eastern extremity of Lake Simcoe and Match-

adash Bay, was recommended by him as essentially necessary;
also approximate profiles of a route through Albion, and from
the Holland river to the Nottawasaga river, which was afterward
formally sanctioned and ordered by the Committee. In conformity
with these suggestions and directions, I have also to submit the
required information in reference to those routes, with the plans
and profiles of the same, without which information the report
could not be said to have been satisfactorily completed.

I have the honor to remain, sir,

Your obedient servant,

KIVAS TULLY.

Thomas Clarkson, Esq.,
    Chairman of the Committee, and President of the Board of Trade, Toronto.

REPORT.

The peculiar outline of the western portion of the Province of
Canada, with respect to the northern boundary line of the United
States, has often been subject to comment by several public writers.
The short distance between the Georgian Bay and Lake Ontario
in the vicinity of Toronto across this western peninsula, compared
with the circuitous route by Lakes Erie and Huron, has long
attracted the attention of those who have taken an interest in
the progress of this section of the province, and suggested this
route as a probable means of water communication with the
north-west.

From the earliest period of the history of this province, the
route from Toronto by Lake Simcoe to the Georgian Bay on Lake
Huron has been known and used as a portage by the Indians and
traders to the north-west, in preference to the routes by the Ottawa
river or Lake Erie. The rapid increase, during the last ten years,
of the population, and, consequent agricultural and commercial
progress of the States of the American Union, lying immediately
west of Lake Michigan, and the serious losses to life, property and
shipping on the St. Clair Flats and Lake Erie, also, the limited
facilities afforded by the Erie canal for the transport of merchan-
dise to and from those western states, have directed the serious
attention of merchants and shipowners in the United States and
Canada to the construction of the Toronto and Georgian Bay Ship
Canal, as an additional avenue for facilitating the internal commercial transport between the west and the seaboard.

It is now nearly twelve years since this route was first explored by me, at the request of Dr. Rees of this city [see appendix to report], but the probable cost of the proposed communication, compared with the prospective trade, prevented any serious discussion on the subject. In fact it was considered altogether chimerical at that time, and beyond the mere exploration, the question was not entertained.

The cost of the extensive excavation that would have to be made through the ridge of land lying between Lakes Simcoe and Ontario, so as to permit the use of the waters of Lake Simcoe as a feeder to the proposed canal, was considered, at that time, to be beyond the demands of the western trade; but the unparalleled rapidity with which this trade has increased during the last ten years, and its undoubted future augmentation, has forced the question prominently on the attention of the mercantile community, and the demand for an additional avenue is now seriously made.

In a letter addressed by me to John B. Robinson, Esq., M. P. P. for this city, a copy of which accompanies this report, I have endeavored to point out the failure of the Welland Canal in diverting the western trade to the River St. Lawrence, as the cheapest route between the north-west portion of this continent and Europe; the consequent demand for the construction of an additional avenue at a more northerly point than Lake Erie, and the superior advantages of this route over all others in reference to distance and anticipated economical working.

I now feel satisfied, from tangible evidence, that the statements there made will be fully borne out and established in this report, and also in that of the Consulting Engineer, Col. R. B. Mason, which is now in course of preparation.

The delay that has occurred in the completion of the survey was unavoidable. I was unwilling that any but reliable information should be presented to the public, as, in the absence of reliable data, the future success of the undertaking might be seriously impeded, and the construction of the canal delayed. In order to present the requisite information in as distinct and satisfactory a manner as possible, the report has been framed under the following heads:

1st. Terminal Harbor accommodation. 2d. Water supply to the canal. 3d. Cost of construction. 4th. Comparison of the routes. 5th. General comparison with other routes. 6th. Collateral advantages. 7th. Conclusion.

I.— TERMINAL HARBOR ACCOMMODATION.

At the convention held in this city on the 13th of September, 1855, to consider the question of the construction of the Georgian Bay Canal, it was unanimously

Resolved, That the immense trade from the North-west demands the immediate construction of a canal between the Upper Lakes and Lake Ontario, of sufficient capacity to pass vessels of 1000 tons burthen from Lake Huron to Lake Ontario at Toronto or its vicinity.

In accordance with the instructions of the committee, Toronto Harbor was made the starting point from Lake Ontario. The survey was commenced immediately west of the old Fort, and the ground between this point and Lambton on the River Humber was accurately measured and leveled. From the Grand Trunk Railway Bridge, where it crosses the River Don, a line was also leveled along the banks of the river and a branch of the Don which crosses Yonge street, immediately north of the city, continuing along the base of the Davenport hill until it joined the western line. The intention of surveying and leveling those lines was to ascertain the approximate elevation of the ground above the level of the Humber River, and otherwise determine the feasibility of constructing both those branches, not only as termini, but also as an available water power, the future advantage of which would be incalculable to the prosperity of this city for manufacturing and ordinary mechanical purposes.

I regret to state that without the expenditure of a much larger amount than will be required to construct the proposed canal by another terminal line, this desirable result cannot be obtained. The principal difficulties to be overcome are the incapacity of the entrance to the harbor of Toronto to permit the passage of vessels of 1000 tons and drawing 12 feet of water, and the necessity of constructing a high dam across the Humber and an aqueduct across the Black Creek at a point about two miles above Weston.

At the lowest water level of Lake Ontario, which must be taken as the datum as far as regards a terminal harbor, there would be only eleven feet of water in the channel at the entrance, and the bottom being rock, could not be deepened, except at considerable expense. As the proposed terminus of the canal would have been to the west of Toronto, in moderate weather only vessels could enter or leave the canal without entering Toronto Harbor, but this is a contingency that should not be risked.

The terminal harbor accommodation for shipping should be safe, easy of access under ordinary circumstances, and commodious. In no respect could this be attained at the proposed terminus west of the Queen's Wharf without the expenditure of a much larger amount than would be necessary if a harbor was constructed elsewhere. The only feasible line by which Toronto Harbor could be made the terminus would be to the east by the valley of the river Don, where the requisite depth of water could be procured at a reasonable cost. This line would require the construction of an eastern entrance at Ashbridge's Bay. To construct a suitable terminal entrance for the proposed Ship Canal, at this place, would require a much larger amount than would be necessary at the mouth of the Humber River for a harbor of a superior character.

Even during the highest water level on Lake Ontario, which would give 16 feet of water on the present entrance to the Toronto harbor, the passage of a vessel of 1000 tons, and drawing 12 feet of water, during a south-westerly gale, would be attended with great risk.

For these reasons I have come to the conclusion that the necessary terminal accommodation cannot be afforded at the harbor of Toronto within a reasonable cost. The explorations and surveys of the several routes demonstrate that the valley of the River Humber is the most direct and practicable line that can be adopted for the southern portion of the canal. The cost of constructing the canal from Weston to the mouth of the River Humber will not be greater than would be necessary under the most favorable circumstances, and would be of an ordinary character, whereas, if the terminus was at Toronto, the apparent cost of the intermediate construction would be much greater, so much so that I have not considered it necessary to encumber the Report with a comparison of the estimates. In addition to the above, the Eastern line, with a terminus at Ashbridge's Bay, would be six miles longer; and the Western line, with a terminus at the Queen's Wharf, two miles longer than the Humber line. Under these circumstances, therefore, I consider the Humber line offers the greatest advantages, and, in recommending this line, the Humber Bay would be assumed as the southern terminal entrance of the canal. By the construction of two piers of crib work, 2,000 feet in length and 40 feet in width, 200 feet apart, and extending into 20 feet of water, with a depth of not less than 13 feet, at low water, inside the piers, a terminal harbor, safe, easy of access, and commodious, can be obtained at the Humber Bay. This bay is protected from the effects of north-westerly, also easterly storms, which are the most violent on Lake Ontario, by the Peninsula, south of Toronto, about 4 miles distant; but there is little or no protection from south-westerly storms, which prevail during the autumn, unless when close to the entrance, which is sheltered by a projecting headland to the west. The distance to the opposite shore of the Lake being only 30 miles, the force of the wave would not be such as to materially endanger the safety of a large vessel running between piers 200 feet apart, and in 20 feet of water, whilst smaller vessels of 500 tons can run into Toronto harbor in safety, during unusually severe gales from this quarter. During the period of low water, the Humber Bay, with the proposed piers, would be the only available terminal harbor for vessels of the capacity for which the canal is proposed to be constructed.

Within the line of shore, after passing between the piers, the marsh is proposed to be excavated to the extent of eight acres, so as to afford sufficient accommodation for the anticipated traffic, and is capable of being enlarged, if required.

For the terminal harbor accommodation on Lake Huron two points have been surveyed — one at the mouth of the Nottawasaga River, and the other at Matchedash or Gloucester Bay. The selection of either of these harbors will, in a great measure, be determined by the choice of routes, but, as respects the amount to be expended on each, the Nottawasaga River requires a less outlay. By the construction of piers, of the same character as those recommended for the Humber Bay, also 200 feet in length, a harbor similar in many respects may be obtained. The mouth of the Nottawasaga River would be exposed to the north-west gales of the Georgian Bay, which are sometimes very violent in the spring and autumn, and would have a range of 100 miles to Cabot's Head.

This would no doubt be a serious difficulty in a nautical point of view, but the risk would not be so hazardous if ordinary caution is used. Supposing a vessel to be running for the entrance of the canal, at the mouth of the Nottawasaga River, the vessel would pass close to the Christian Islands, under the lee of which shelter could be procured until the severity of the storm had passed, when the entrance of the harbor, 29 miles distant, could be reached in safety.

This course would not be necessary during ordinary gales, but only in case of unusually severe storms. With this exception, Nottawasaga Bay offers every facility for a suitable terminal harbor, the approach being marked with bold headlands, and with deep water one mile from the shore.

For the better explanation of the capabilities of this river and the Humber as terminal harbors, I have prepared detailed charts of the same, which are herewith submitted. By reference to the chart of the Nottawasaga River, which has been drawn from actual survey, it will be noticed that the river extends in a south-westerly direction parallel to the line of the shore for a distance of nearly 3 miles, with a width varying from 220 feet to 650 feet, and an average depth of 10 feet, containing available harbor accommodation of over 150 acres, at a moderate outlay for deepening and improvement, the cost of which is stated in the general estimate.

Gloucester Bay, through which a vessel would pass to Matchedash Bay, being what is termed land-locked, would, in the case of sailing vessels, be objectionable on account of its being too much sheltered; but this would not affect steam propellors.

In order to render Matchedash Bay available as a terminal harbor, it would be necessary to dredge a channel one hundred feet wide through the center, for nearly four miles, and also to remove a large quantity of granite boulders. This latter work would be attended with a considerable and unavoidable expense, the approximate cost of which is given in the general estimate.

On this account, I consider this bay inferior to the Nottawasaga river, as a terminal harbor, and am therefore strongly in favor of the latter.

I am aware that strong objections have been urged successfully against the practicability of forming and maintaining a harbor at the mouth of the Nottawasaga river. I cannot agree with such opinions, and would here mention that on my first inspection of this harbor, in company with Col. Mason, the consulting engineer, more than two years since, I did not hesitate to express my belief that a safe and commodious harbor could be constructed at this point, superior to many of the harbors on the lakes, with which Col. Mason agreed; and I am satisfied he has not since changed his opinion. In fact, we were both fully convinced that an industrious and populous city would sooner or later spring up on the banks of the river and the narrow peninsular which divides it from the bay.

3

II. — WATER SUPPLY TO THE CANAL.

The proposed dimensions of the locks are 265 feet in length, 55 feet in width, 12 feet lift, and 12 feet on the sill.

Two locks of these dimensions would require 350,000 cubic feet of water, nearly, for each vessel passing through the canal. If 500 vessels passed through during the day, 17,500,000 cubic feet would be required, or about 12,000 cubic feet per minute. According to two experiments on the quantity of water flowing from Lake Simcoe into Lake Couchiching, at the narrows, the quantity of water at this point amounted to over 100,000 cubic feet per minute, making due allowance for the friction at the bottom and sides.

The average rain fall of the water shed of Lake Simcoe (1,200 square miles), according to a statement procured from the Meteorological Observatory, at Toronto [*See Appendix C.*], and extending over a period of seventeen years, gives 36.94 inches; and allowing for evaporation, absorption and vegetation, say 24.94 inches, we have twelve inches available rain fall per square foot for the year. This would give 90,000,000 per day, or 60,000 per minute. The available supply would be greater than this, judging by the experiments at the narrows, which give over 100,000 cubic feet per minute. According to experiments in the county of Hertford, in England, the evaporative effect was as 15 to 27, nearly, or a little above 50 per cent., leaving $33\frac{1}{3}$ per cent. additional to be consumed by vegetation. What the exact amount of loss from this cause is, cannot be ascertained; but the sum of both would hardly exceed two-thirds of the whole rain fall, which would be five times as much as would be required to pass fifty vessels, of 1,000 tons each, per day, as this would be the greatest number of vessels that could be passed through the canal conveniently in fifteen hours, allowing a little over fifteen minutes for each vessel to pass through the locks. There will still be a large available water power, which, along the entire line of the canal, after passing the summit level, will form a source of considerable future profit, by renting the same for mills and manufactories.

Immediately after passing the summit, an additional water power would be also available from the water sheds of the Humber and Nottawasaga rivers, amounting to 30,000 cubic feet per minute, and 52,000 cubic feet per minute respectively along the line of the canal, based on the same calculations of an average of twelve inches per superficial foot per annum. Further evidence is hardly necessary, and from the above sources there will not only be a sufficient supply of water to feed the canal, but a large remaining available water power; in fact, an inexhaustible supply for the wants of a much more numerous population than can be anticipated at present.

In order to store up the rain fall of the Lake Simcoe water shed, it will be necessary to construct one waste weir and three close dams at the branches of the river Severn, at the north-eastern extremity of lake Couchiching, the cost of which is stated in the general estimate.

III.—COST OF CONSTRUCTION.

This question also embraces the practicability of the construction of the several proposed routes.

The route, as originally agreed on, commenced at "Toronto or its vicinity," passed along the valley of the Humber, in a northerly direction, through the township of Kings, to the Holland river and Cook's Bay, on Lake Simcoe; from thence to Kempenfeldt Bay, or the western shore of Lake Simcoe. The starting point from Kempenfeldt Bay was from the mouth of a creek about one mile from Barrie, at the extremity of the bay, thence in a westerly direction to the Nottawasaga river, about one mile north of the Ontario, Simcoe and Huron railway line, and following the valley of the river to the Nottawasaga Bay, the most southerly portion of the Georgian Bay, Lake Huron.

ROUTE NO. ONE.

The terminal harbor accommodation having been already considered, it is only necessary to describe the extent and character of the works to be executed between the termini.

Along the valley of the Humber there are no engineering difficulties of an extraordinary character as far as the 23d section, at the town line of Vaughan and King, where the deep excavation through the ridges commences. This excavation extends to the 33d section, or ten miles. The greatest depth to be excavated will be 137.76

feet, or 2.24 under 200 feet. This will be the greatest depth from
the summit. The ridges present a gradual inclination north and
south; the slope to the north being 5½ miles in length, and the
southern slope 4½ miles; total length 10 miles. The depth of this
excavation will average 90 feet, and will contain nearly 48,000,000
cubic yards, and being composed, as far as can be conjectured, of
light clay and gravel, will not cost more than 25 cents per yard,
making a total of $12,000,000. From the 33d section to the 48th,
to Cook's Bay, at Lake Simcoe, the canal would pass through the
Holland River marsh, following the course of the Holland River,
except at the bends of the river, which are cut off. A considerable
portion of this river is of an available capacity, and would require
slight alterations, averaging 150 feet in width, with a depth of
water from 9 to 12 feet.

From the 48th to the 71st section, at the western extremity of
Kempenfeldt Bay, it will be lake navigation where there are no difficulties to be encountered; Lake Simcoe being of sufficient capacity
to admit vessels of a large tonnage navigating it without any risk.
At the 48th and 71st sections piers of timber crib work of a suitable character have to be constructed.

From section No. 1 to No. 6 there will be a deep excavation
averaging 50 feet, the greatest depth at section No. 2 being 78 feet,
and containing a little over 6,000,000 cubic yards at twenty-five cents
per cubic yard, the total cost of which would be $1,500,000 — the
material to be excavated being of the same quality as described in
the deep excavation in the ridges as far as can be judged from
geological data, and other indications. [*See Appendix D.*]

At section No. 8, the character of the work comprises a chain
of combination locks six in number. From this section to No. 25,
there are no engineering difficulties, as the canal will follow the
course of the Nottawasaga River, which, with slight improvements,
can be rendered of sufficient capacity to answer the required purposes. This portion, 16 miles in length, being liable to heavy
floods in the Spring and Autumn, will require a much higher towpath than usual, which will slightly increase the average cost per
mile. Between the 25th and the 27th sections, it will be necessary
to cut a channel through the sand ridge which forms the south-
eastern bank of the Nottawasaga Harbor, in order to save a distance
of six miles, a waste weir being constructed across the river to
maintain the water at the required level.

The total quantity contained in this excavation will be over 2,000,000 cubic yards, the greatest depth being 100 feet, and the average depth 50 feet; the cost of this excavation would be $500,000.

From the 27th to the 29th section the work would consist of dredging the bed of the river of an average depth of two feet. The 29th section reaches the Nottawasaga Bay, where a harbor is to be constructed as before described.

The lockage on route No. 1 will consist of two single locks, eight double locks, three treble locks, and three quadruple combination locks, being thirty-nine locks in number from Lake Ontario to Lake Simcoe, having an average lift of a little over 12 feet, and the total lockage of 470 feet.

From Kempenfeldt Bay to Lake Huron there will be five single locks, and six combination locks, or altogether eleven locks, with an average lift of a little under 12 feet, or 130 feet in all—making the total lockage of route No. 1 to be 600 feet.

In nearly every instance where combination locks have been provided, it was a matter of necessity from the nature of the surface. Though objectionable in many respects, it is of advantage in consequence of increasing the length of the levels, which on this route will vary from 1 to 16 miles, not including the long summit level of Lake Simcoe of 56 miles. The total length of this route will be 100 statute miles.

The canal, if constructed by this route, would cross the Great Western and Grand Trunk Railways, and the Ontario, Simcoe and Huron Railway twice. At each of these points as indicated on the map, a railway swing bridge must be constructed. Accommodation swing bridges of an ordinary character will have to be constructed at several points along the route. For crossing the deep excavation it is proposed to have four accommodation bridges 20 feet above the level of the water, with inclined approaches of 1 in 20, each bridge to be two miles apart for the entire length.

***

ROUTE NO. TWO,

Comprises the first portion of route No. 1, between Lakes Ontario and Simcoe.

The continuation of this line extends from the terminus on Lake Simcoe to Dr. Robinson's creek, on the north-west shore of Lake

Couchiching, at the north-eastern extremity of Lake Simcoe, about midway between the "Narrows and the River Severn." The distance from Lake Ontario to this point being eighty-one miles, from section 48 to 81, comprises Lake Simcoe, the only difficult portion of the navigation being at the Narrows, which consists of a circuitous and hazardous channel. The Board of Public Works of the Province has ordered the necessary improvements, which have been in course of execution during the past year, rendering any additional expenditure unnecessary, except the contingency of deepening the channel still more, as the present improvement only contemplated accommodation for steam vessels drawing eight or nine feet of water.

From Dr. Robinson's creek to Matchedash Bay the canal would be fourteen miles in length.

Between sections Nos. 1 and 4, a deep excavation will be necessary, principally through limestone rock, containing over 5,500,000 cubic yards, at a cost of the same amount in dollars, the cost of excavation being estimated at $1 per cubic yard. The greatest depth would be 138 feet, and the average depth 75 feet. From section No. 4 to No. 8, the construction is of an ordinary character; between Nos. 8 and 9 an excavation, also through limestone rock, occurs, containing 500,000 cubic yards, and at section No. 13 an excavation through granite, containing 300,000 cubic yards, at a cost of at least $3 per cubic yard. Between sections 14 and 17 (Matchedash Bay) a channel will have to be excavated 100 feet in width, and a trackway in crib work constructed; the quantity of excavation, a large portion of which would be through granite, would be nearly 1,000,000 cubic yards, the cost of which would be $3,250,000, including the cost of the trackway and harbor accommodation.

The lockage on route No. 2, consists of six single locks, one double, and one treble combination lock—11 locks altogether, the lift being the same as for Route No. 1, between Lake Simcoe and Lake Huron, and the total lockage 600 feet.

The total distance by this route, denominated No. 2, combining a portion of No. 1, would be 98 miles, comprising 63 miles of summit level, including Lake Simcoe, and levels ranging in length from one quarter of a mile to 30 miles.

The cost of bridging on route No. 2, not including the combined portion of No. 1, would be trifling, as the country through which the canal would pass, is unsettled, excepting portions at the termini

A trackway of timber crib work, 20 feet in width, and three miles in length, must be constructed on the east side of the channel, to be excavated through Matchedash Bay; also harbor accommodation at the entrance on Gloucester Bay.

ROUTE NO. THREE,

Comprises a portion of No. 1, as far as the 14th section, from which point it branches off to the west, through t'e valley of the north-west branch of the Humber and the township of Albion, and the valley of the Nottawasaga River, in Tecumseth and Essa, where it again joins route No. 1, at section No. 10, and continues along this line to the terminal harbor, at the mouth of the Nottawasaga River.

The deepest excavation on this route occurs between sections Nos. 13 and 28, containing 114,000,000 cubic yards, which would cost $28,500,000, and the greatest depth to 246 feet, an amount which places this route, beyond all comparison, the most expensive.

It was considered necessary to arrive at some approximate estimate of the cost of this route, as several persons living in the township of Albion were under the impression that this was the most direct and cheapest route for the canal.

The cost of the necessary excavation, as stated above, will, as a matter of course, completely remove this impression. In addition to this cost, a feeder from Lake Simcoe would require to be constructed. The lockage would be the same as No. 1, and the length would be 83 miles.

ROUTE NO. FOUR,

Comprises the principal portion of No. 1, as far as section No. 35, where it branches off from the Holland River through North Gwillimbury and Tecumseth toward the Nottawassaga River, where it joins route No. 3, at section 32.

This was one of the routes approved and recommended by Col. Mason to the committee in 1855, and will be found to possess many superior advantages in comparison with other routes.

This route, like No. 3, does not enter Lake Simcoe, though it is proposed to be connected with it by a navigable feeder adapted for a smaller class of vessels. The greatest amount of excavation on this route occurs between sections Nos. 2 and 8, containing 8,000,000 cubic yards, which would cost 2,000,000, the greatest depth being 123 feet, and the average depth 64 feet.

From section 32 of route No. 3, to section No. 10 of route No. 1, where No. 3 joins, there are no constructive difficulties, as the fall in the valley of the Nottawasaga river is comparatively trifling for the whole of this distance (eighteen miles). The line then continues along route No. 1 to the terminal harbor at the mouth of the Nottawsaga river. The lockage on this route will be the same as No. 1 (600 feet), and the distance 84 miles. Several accommodation bridges will be required on this route.

ESTIMATE OF COST.

Subjoined are the estimates of the cost of the proposed routes, route No. 1 being the least, and route No. 3 the greatest, the difference between Nos. 1 and 2 being trifling.

The cost of the harbor accommommodation of No. 2, is the largest, and Nos. 3 and 4 the least. It will also be observed, that in the construction of route No. 3 a much larger amount of excavation would be required than in the other routes, and next in order Nos. 4 and 2. The size of the locks has been determined by the dimensions of the propeller "Iowa" of 1,000 tons, namely, 242 feet long, $31\frac{1}{3}$ feet wide, and drawing $11\frac{1}{2}$ feet of water when loaded; making allowance for the necessary space for opening and closing the gates, locks 265 feet in length, 55 feet in width and 12 feet on the sill, are considered sufficient for the purpose. Two schooners of 400 tons each can also pass through locks of these dimensions at the same time.

The canal is intended to be 115 feet wide at the water line, and 13 feet in depth, except in the deep excavation, where the width at the water line is proposed to be 100 feet, and through the rock cutting on route No. 2, 90 feet at the water level and 100 feet above the level of the towpath.

The greatest width of the deep excavation through the ridges in King, would be 680 feet at the surface level.

ESTIMATE OF ROUTE No. 1.

QUANTITY.	DESCRIPTION OF WORK.	RATE.	DOLLS.
63,300,000 c yds.	Earth excavation	25c	$15,825,000
	50 locks complete............	$80,000	4,000,000
	4 dams....................	5,000	20,000
	25 waste weirs	4,000	100,000
	2 harbor accommodations	200,000	400,000
	2 harbor Lake Simcoe........	100,000	200,000
	50 accommodation bridges	5,000	250,000
	15 culverts	8,000	120,000
	Land damages..............		200,000
			$21,115,000
	Engineering and contingencies		1,055,750
			$22,170,750

ESTIMATE OF ROUTE No. 2.

QUANTITY.	DESCRIPTION OF WORK.	RATE.	DOLLS.
54,000,000 c. yds.	Earth excavation	25c	$13,500,000
6,000,000 "	Rock excavation, limestone....	$1 00	6,000,000
700,000 "	Rock excavation, granite......	3 00	2,100,000
	Locks.....................		4,000,000
	Dams		20,000
	Waste weirs		100,000
	Harbor accommodation		600,000
	" " Lake Simcoe..		200,000
	Bridges		200,000
	Culverts..................		100,000
	Land damages.......		200,000
			$27,020,000
	Engineering and contingencies.		1,351,000
			$28,371,000

ESTIMATE OF ROUTE No. 3.

QUANTITY.	DESCRIPTION OF WORK.	RATE.	DOLLS.
135,000,000 c. y'ds.	Earth excavation including feeder	25c	$33,750,000
	Locks		4,000,000
	Dams.....................		20,000
	Waste Weirs................		100,000
	Harbor accommodations........		400,000
	Bridges...................		250,000
	Culverts..................		120,000
	Land damages..............		200,000
			$38,840,000
	Engineering and contingencies..		2,192,000
			$41,032,000

ESTIMATE OF ROUTE No. 4.

QUANTITY.	DESCRIPTION OF WORK.	RATE.	DOLLS.
70,000,000 c. y'ds.	Earth excavation..............	25c	$17,500,000
	Locks.......................		4,000,000
	Dams.......................		20,000
	Waste Weirs.................		100,000
	Harbor accommodation.........		400,000
	Bridges.....		250,000
	Culverts.....................		120,000
	Land damages...............		200,000
			$22,590,000
	Engineering and contingencies..		1,129,500
			$23,719,500

COMPARISON OF THE ROUTES.

With respect to the terminal harbor accommodation, routes Nos. 1, 3 and 4 are on an equality, and would, in my opinion, be superior to No. 2, the terminal harbor of which would be at Matchedash Bay. Beside the difficulty of constructing a channel through Matchedash Bay, there would be a great risk to vessels drifting aground, not only on the west side of the channel, during easterly winds, but also in Gloucester Bay. On the east side there are several large granite boulders, to remove which, and construct a trackway on the west side of the channel, through Matchedash Bay, would add nearly $1,000,000 more to the estimate. As a harbor of refuge, the west side of Gloucester Bay would be superior in every respect, and would afford the most ample accommodation for all classes of vessels during the season of navigation. For sailing vessels it is rather too much sheltered, but for propellors it would be accessible at all times.

In the early portion of the spring, and late in the autumn, its sheltered waters would also be frozen at least one week sooner, the entrance to the harbor being nearly half a degree further north than the proposed terminal harbor at the Nottawasaga River. For general traffic I would, therefore, recommend the other routes in preference to No. 2, for terminal harbor accommodation. The comparative cost of the route is as follows:

No. 1..$22,170,750
No. 2.. 22,596,000
No. 3.. 41,032,000
No. 4.. 23,719,500

The details are stated in the estimate. With regard to cost, No. 1 route is most favorable. The difference between Nos. 1, 2 and 4 cannot be considered sufficient to give one route a very great advantage over the other in this respect; but the cost of route No. 3, being double, precludes any further argument in its favor. The comparison, therefore, between Nos. 1, 2 and 4 will be narrowed to the question of facilities of construction and economical working. The heavy amount of rock excavation encountered in route No. 2 appears objectionable on account of the increased price, but the quantity being much less on account of the side slopes being decreased, the difference of cost will not be so great as stated in the estimate.

The limestone to be excavated being of a quality that could be used in the construction of the locks on this section of the route, if not on others, would diminish the cost of this excavation. As this is, in a great measure, a matter of conjecture, no deduction has been made in the estimate on this account, particularly as it is probable that the stone required for building the locks on the remaining sections would be procured from other localities.

The question of terminal harbor accommodation and cost having been decided, that of economical working has next to be considered. The lockage being the same on all the routes, the length of the routes and time occupied in passing through the canal, will determine the superiority. The respective lengths and time will be as follows:

ROUTE.	LENGTH IN MILES.				TIME IN HOURS.		
	Lake Simcoe.	Summit.	Other levels.	Total.	Canals.	Locks.	Total.
Route No. 1.........................	23	33	44	100	37	16	53
Route No. 2.........................	33	30	35	98	33	16	49
Route No. 3.........................	..	23	60	83	38	16	54
Route No. 4.........................	..	26	58	84	38	16	54

In the above calculations, the rate of speed on Lake Simcoe is calculated at six miles per hour, on the summit three miles, and two miles on the other levels. Nearly twenty minutes is allowed for passing each lock.

The comparison in time would be in favor of route No. 2. The terminal harbor accommodation, being in favor of Nos. 1 and 4, will give them a greater advantage, according to my judgment.

The comparison, therefore, will rest between these two latter routes. In point of time, then, the difference is of no consideration; the principal and final objection to route No. 1 would be the probable delay to sailing vessels passing through Lake Simcoe in consequence of adverse winds, to which No. 4 would not be subject.

Would this inconvenience, or consequent expense, be at all in proportion to the difference between the cost of the routes, namely, $1,500,000? I think not; and I am the more inclined to this decision from the certainty that the majority of the vessels passing through the canal would be propellers, which would not be affected by adverse winds; at least, it would not prevent their continuing their passage through Lake Simcoe, or, in fact, from either terminus, except during very severe storms.

Under all the circumstances of comparison, the route as originally proposed, appears to be the best, and I am not aware that any further local examination would alter this decision, as, in every instance, I am satisfied that the most favorable locality was selected. In any comparison, therefore, with other, or existing, or proposed avenues for the western trade, the route from the river Humber, west of Toronto, to Lake Simcoe, and from thence to Lake Huron, by the Nottawassago river, will only be considered.

The estimated cost being................................... $22,170,750
The length.. .... 100 miles.
And the time.. 53 hours.

V. — GENERAL COMPARISON WITH OTHER ROUTES.

The existing water communications between Lakes Superior, Michigan and Huron, and the Atlantic Ocean, are as follows:

No. 1 — By Lake Erie, Buffalo and Erie Canal.
No. 2 —   "   "   Welland Canal, and Oswego and Erie Canal.
No. 3 —   "   "   "   "   and the St. Lawrence.

The projected water communications, as ship canals, are:

No. 1 — By Lake Erie, Welland Canal and St. Lawrence.
No. 2 — By Georgian Bay, Toronto and St. Lawrence.
No. 3 — By   "   "   Ottawa River and St. Lawrence.

To which may be added the proposed ship canal between the St. Lawrence, Lake Champlain, and the river Hudson, and from Oswego to the river Hudson. Nos. 1 and 2 of the existing routes have New York as their sea port, and No. 3 Montreal and Quebec.

For the projected routes, New York, Montreal and Quebec would be the sea ports, in case the projected ship canals between Montreal and Oswego and the Hudson river were constructed, and the St. Lawrence canal enlarged.

Chicago being the center of internal commerce at present, will, in every comparison, be made the starting point, and *vice versa*.

This city must be selected as the starting point from the west, for obvious reasons. The rapid growth of Chicago in all those elements which constitute a great commercial and enterprising city, indicating, as it does, a prosperity and progress unparalleled in the commercial history of the world, justifies the well earned title of the "Center of Western Commerce."

The cities of Milwaukee and Superior, also Waukegan, Kenosha, Sheboygan and Green Bay, are proportionably interested in the construction of this additional avenue for their trade, and will no doubt unite with Chicago and Canada in ensuring its accomplishment.

A division of interests in advocating the construction of other channels for western trade, until this is completed, would be fatal to the success not only of this project, but of all others which are designed to facilitate the transit of western commerce.

Comparative Distances and Estimated Time of the Existing and Proposed Routes.

FROM CHICAGO TO NEW YORK.

No.	ROUTE.	DISTANCE IN MILES.			Lockage, height in feet.	TIME IN HOURS.				REMARKS.
		River and Lake.	Canal.	Total.		River and Lake.	Canal.	Lockage	Total.	
1	Buffalo, Erie canal and Hudson river	1,251	364	1,615	692	156	121	17	294	The distance from Chicago to Buffalo, is taken at 1,100 miles, and from Chicago to the Georgian Bay at 600 miles. See report on Ottawa route, W. Shanly, C. E.
2	Welland, Oswego canal and the Hudson river	1,401	237	1,638	1,040	175	79	26	280	
3	Welland, Champlain canal and the Hudson river	1,682	164	1,846	633	210	55	16	281	
4	Georgian Bay, Toronto, Oswego and the Hudson river	924	286	1,210	1,310	115	95	33	244	
5	Georgian Bay, Toronto, St. Lawrence and the Hudson river	1,205	213	1,418	903	150	71	23	244	
6	Georgian Bay, Ottawa and the Hudson river	1,078	300	1,378	924	135	100	23	258	

FROM CHICAGO TO QUEBEC.

No.	ROUTE.	DISTANCE IN MILES.			Lockage, height in feet.	TIME IN HOURS.				REMARKS.
		River and Lake.	Canal.	Total.		River and Lake.	Canal.	Lockage	Total.	
1	Welland and St. Lawrence river	1,593	71	1,664	535	199	24	13	236	For comparison of distances. See Board of Works (Canada) Report, 1857.
2	Georgian Bay, Toronto and St. Lawrence	1,116	120	1,236	805	140	40	20	200	
3	Georgian Bay, Ottawa and St. Lawrence	973	212	1,185	681	122	70	17	209	

N. B.—In the above tables, for steam propellers, eight miles an hour is allowed for the rate of speed on the river and lake, three miles an hour on the canal, and one and a half minutes for every foot of lockage.

New York to Liverpool, 2,980 miles; Quebec to Liverpool, 2,502 miles; difference in favor of Quebec, 478 miles.

By the above table of comparative distances, it will be perceived that the Toronto and Georgian Bay Canal would not only be the shortest of existing or proposed routes in distance, with one exception, but allowing for the increased lockage, would also be the shortest in point of time, whether New York or Quebec is the seaport. By a comparison with the shortest of existing routes to New York, namely, Buffalo, Erie canal and Hudson river, the Toronto, Georgian Bay and Oswego route would be 405 miles and about four days shorter in point of time, allowing fifteen working hours for each day during the season of navigation.

Also, by comparing the Welland and St. Lawrence to Quebec, with the Toronto, Georgian Bay and St. Lawrence, the latter would have an advantage of 428 miles in distance and save over three days. In the above calculations the detention in passing the St. Clair Flats are not taken into consideration, which, according to the argument in favor of the construction of the Rondeau and Chatham Ship canal, averaged six days for each trip, or three days either way. The average annual losses to shipping at this point alone, irrespective of detention, has been calculated at $1,000,000, which would be so much saved and in favor of the Toronto and Georgian Bay route. On this basis a comparison may be formed between the above and any of the other routes, and in every instance it will be found to be still more favorable.

The difference, also, from Chicago to Liverpool by the Georgian Bay, Toronto and Quebec, is 452 miles less than by Toronto, Oswego and New York, and 857 miles than by the present route by Buffalo, Erie canal and Hudson river.

If it is admitted that the time has now arrived when Ship Canals must be constructed to connect the great lakes with the Atlantic Ocean, then the Toronto and Georgian Bay route possesses still further advantages over all others existing or projected. The expense and difficulty of deepening St. Clair Flats from $9\frac{1}{2}$ to 12 feet, and, it may be added, impracticability, except at a considerable expense, would be an effectual barrier which could only be removed by the construction of the Rondeau and Chatham Ship Canal, at this point, at an estimated cost of $6,000,000. The proposed lateral cut to the Welland Canal has also been estimated at $4,000,000. There we have a proposed expenditure of

$10,000,000 of Canadian capital, which, if expended in the construction of the Toronto and Georgian Bay Ship Canal, would leave but $12,000,000 to complete a work which would save 428 miles by the Quebec route, including the hazardous navigation on Lake Erie, which is admitted to be the most disastrous compared with all the other lakes.

The tendency of the construction of the Rondeau and Chatham Ship Canal, the most feasible and economical method by which the navigation of this portion of the St. Lawrence can be improved, would be to facilitate the existing trade to and from Buffalo and the Erie Canal; the proportion of the increase of trade to the Welland Canal and St. Lawrence could hardly be expected to be at all commensurate with the cost of the undertaking as far as this Province would be concerned.

Since 1847, "when the rivalry for the carrying trade of the great west was fairly begun between Canada and the State of New York," the expected trade by the St. Lawrence has been gradually diminishing in comparison with the Erie Canal. During the approaching season the enlarged Erie Canal will offer increased facilities for western traffic, and the trade of the St. Lawrence will be still further reduced. It has been truly remarked that "all the canals, railways, and other means of communication that can be made across the Canadian peninsula for the next twenty years, will not afford sufficient accommodation for the gigantic increase of the commerce of the great West." Admitting the truth of the above remark, it would be inconsistent to oppose any of the projected improvements either by Buffalo or Montreal, but the superior claim that this route has on Canadians should be first considered, and our energies directed to its early completion. If its construction will restore the trade to the St. Lawrence that has been lost, then we ought firmly to protest against Canadian influence and capital being expended on rival projects.

With respect to the capacity of the proposed Toronto and Georgian Bay Canal, in comparison with those of existing routes, it will be conceded at once to be superior in every respect.

The passage of 50 vessels per day of 1000 tons each, or 10,000,000 tons in 200 days, which is the estimated yearly period of navigation, would meet the requirements of the trade for some years to come, while the present traffic, about 6,000,000 tons, is quite as much as the Erie Canal can conveniently accommodate,

and the annual increase will continually demand further enlarge-
ment until at length a ship canal of the proposed dimensions in
this locality will be required.

Instead of this questionable method of occasional enlarge-
ment, the most expensive that can be adopted, would it not be
more advisable to construct additional avenues, thereby creating
increased facilities for internal transports? This, under all circumstances, would appear the reasonable conclusion, and which, it is to
be hoped, will yet be arrived at by all parties interested.

VI. — COLLATERAL ADVANTAGES.

The direct advantages that will follow the construction of the
Toronto and Georgian Bay Ship Canal in opening a shorter and
more expeditious route between Lakes Superior, Michigan and
Huron and the Atlantic Ocean, has been argued in the foregoing
general comparison of routes.

The collateral advantages may be considered as being of a
strictly local character, though their connection with the main
project will become more evident as an auxiliary, when the work
has been completed.

According to the calculations of the available water supply, it
has been computed at 60,000 cubic feet per minute; this supply
from the summit to the north and south would be augmented by
the rain fall of the water sheds of the Humber and Nottawasaga
rivers, which is computed at 82,000 cubic feet per minute, making
a total of 202,000 cubic feet per minute, or 90,000 cubic feet for
the southern or Humber portion, and 112,000 for the northern or
Nottawassaga water shed.

These quantities multiplied by the height, 130 feet for the
northern, and 470 feet for the southern, would give the available
water power of each, an unfailing source of considerable profit,
being in the vicinity of a populous city, and of incalculable value
for manufacturing and mechanical purposes.

CONCLUSION.

In order to convey a clear idea of the position and advantages
of the proposed canal, lithographed plans and profiles are now in

course of preparation, having been reduced from the original plans and profiles which accompany this report.

The first map will represent the united counties of York and Peel, and the county of Simcoe, on which the proposed routes are indicated. The second plan will contain reduced profiles of the routes, and the position and number of the locks.

The last will be a prospectus map, showing the general position of the proposed ship canal to connect Lakes Huron and Ontario at Toronto, in reference to Chicago, New York and Quebec, with the existing and proposed routes and comparative distances before mentioned.

As soon as Col. R. B. Mason's report is completed, it is proposed to have it printed, together with this report, appendix, and plans attached, so as to present the whole in a complete form, and convey the requisite information in as concise a manner as possible, consistent with the importance of the project.

The advantage of having a correct representation of the topography of the country lying between this city and Lake Huron, with the lines of the water sheds of Lake Simcoe, and the Humber and Nottawasaga rivers, will be evident on the inspection of the plans, and has influenced the committee in incurring this additional outlay, which they feel certain will be reimbursed.

The estimated cost of this undertaking will at first appear considerable; but on consideration of the immense advantages that will result from its construction, in comparison with the other public works not yet completed in this Province and the United States, will on serious reflection justify the expenditure of a much larger amount than may have been anticipated when the project was first contemplated.

The cost of the Grand Trunk Railway when complete, including that superior engineering work, the Victoria Bridge at Montreal, has been estimated at $48,000,000, more than double the estimate cost of the canal. This railway, extending from Portland to Stratford, a distance of 714 miles, the remaining portion between Statford and Sarnia, 79 miles, is expected to be completed this year in connection with a railway across the peninsula of Michigan, thereby forming another link between the Atlantic and Great West. The cost of this railway has ceased to be considered a serious matter in comparison to the anticipated advantages; it is now an established fact; the voice of the Legislature having stamped it a notional undertaking, and as such deserving the active and zealous support of the Province generally, to which it has already been indirectly of incalculable advantage by increasing the facilities of communication; it has promoted the agricultural and commercial interests of the community, in some instances more than quadrupled the value of real estate, and laid the foundation of future prosperity and independence.

If these are worthy objects of ambition to a new country like Canada, they should be upheld by the unanimous voice of the Province; if not, let us retrograde to our log shanties, corduroy roads and antiquated conveyances. By way of contrast, I would mention that the journey between Toronto and Coburg, which was formally warranted to be "through by day-light," a distance of 75 miles, occupied 24 hours in its accomplishment, under difficulties of no ordinary description; to this I can personally testify having "gone through by daylight" by mail, and duly arrived next morning about the same time at which we started the previous morning. This occurred in the Autumn of 1847; last Autumn I traveled to Cobourg and returned the same day in seven hours, having seven hours to spare for the transaction of business, and went "through by daylight" in reality, not by fiction.

The immense traffic on the Great Western Railway during the Autumn of 1856 [last year can hardly be considered even an average by which this travel can be estimated], would impress a careful observer with some idea of the extent of the western trade. This railway was also constructed as an additional avenue, and its success as a profitable speculation is undoubted, and its advantages fully admitted by the stockholders. Several other lines are projected to pass through Canada, as competitors with the above-mentioned railways; and on the south shore of Lake Erie, in connection with the Michigan Central Railway, also commands a large share of western traffic. These remarks may be considered foreign to the subject, but in every instance they are forcible illustrations of the magnitude of the western trade. It is needless here to refer to the extent and prospective increase of this trade; it is well understood and appreciated by those who are interested in its developements; it will be considered sufficient to remark, and it is not unreasonable to suppose, judging by the past, that before the Toronto and Georgian Bay Canal can be constructed, the trade of the west may demand a superior capacity of locks, and greater facilities than those at present contemplated. The retention of the trade of the west by the Erie Canal, notwithstanding the continual expenditure and additional facilities annually afforded by the St. Lawrence route, is forcibly commented on by the Hon. John Young in his letter to the Hon. F. Lemieux, Chief Commissioner of Public Works. He states :

"It would be easy to multiply facts to establish the same general results ; but the figures above given will sufficiently show that which we can neither deny nor controvert, namely, *that the trade in the lower St. Lawrence, in the produce of the West, is paltry and insignificant compared with what it ought to be, and compared with that by the Erie Canal;* that our present facilities for transporting property are wholly inadequate to secure successful competition with the more southern route. It is in vain to overlook or undervalue the result; it is forced upon us every year more and more plainly, and was foreseen by every intelligent merchant acquainted with the Western business, and is corroborated by other facts."

In the latter part of 1855, the route by the Ottawa was procured as a panacea for this sickly trade, after the proceedings in Toronto had become public. Lake Nipissing, the proposed feeder of the Ottawa Canal, being two degrees further north than the northern terminus of the Toronto and Georgian Bay Canal, the period of traffic each season of navigation on the Ottawa route would be diminished at least 14 days in the spring and autumn, or one month on an average; and to this may be added the inconveniences of a close navigation for 430 miles, between Lake Huron and the St. Lawrence, as contrasted with 77 miles by this route. For these reasons, and a want of sufficient data in other respects, a comparison may be excused. The terminus of the Ottawa route on Lake Huron will be too far north to compete with the Erie Canal, and, on the contrary, the Welland Canal is too far south. The Toronto and Georgian Bay Canal, being in a direct line between the direct points of traffic, namely, New York on the south-east, and the juncture of the three lakes, Superior, Michigan and Huron, on the north-west, would, if constructed, possess superior advantages in this respect. In the "Prize Essay" on Canada, written by J. S. Hogan, Esq., M. P. P. for the county of Grey, the comparison between the facilities of the St. Lawrence and Erie Canal routes is so clearly described that it is thought advisable to copy it in full, by permission :

"Measuring the St. Lawrence, then, as a highway to the ocean, by the standard that if it can be superseded by more rapid, cheaper, or more convenient routes, it cannot be successful. If it does not fall into disuse, what are its future prospects?

"The first thing that strikes one, in contemplating it, is its adaptation, in point of immensity, to the vast regions it waters. Whilst the business necessities of the West, and those portions of America which are universally admitted to be, both by their relative position to other rivers and to it, its natural feeders, have literally shamed the enterprises that were intended to provide for them, its vast magnitude and its value are being but discovered by the contrast. The Erie Canal, highly valuable as a work, and successful beyond comparison, *has been made little by progress.*

"The St. Lawrence, on the contrary, only requires enormous use to test its greatness. It is impossible, indeed, to contemplate this river, in connection with the canal that was made to rival it, without being struck with the inadequacy of the one and the amplitude of the other.

"The valleys and plains watered by the St. Lawrence, being largely in the United States, have chiefly contributed to the Erie Canal's business. Their fruits were literally wooed away from their natural channel to minister to its prosperity. The St. Lawrence, in so far as American policy, and great restrictions upon commerce, could affect it, has been sacrificed to the Erie Canal. Nature's outlet had navigation laws, which drove commerce away from it, to contend against. The Erie Canal had all these disadvantages to the river converted into advantages in its favor. Yet the laws of progress, which have swept away the obnoxious navigation restrictions, have, at the same time, established the failure of the Erie Canal. Not that it is unprosperous as an enterprise, nor that, *as a local work*, it is not unsurpassed as a speculation, but that, for the great purposes of its construction, namely, to convey to the ocean the fruits and productions of the West and North-west, it is emphatically a failure, *because progress has completely overburthened it; it is literally surfeited by its own prosperity.* And it matters not to him—an individual, in such a case, being the nation—who has boards or flour to send eastward by it, whether they are stopped by reason of starvation, or because of a surfeit. The impediment to his business is the all-important question with him. And though the Erie Canal paid larger profits than any other work in the world, yet, in a national point of view, if it afforded not adequate facilities for business, or stopped it in its course, it might, by drawing to it what it could not do, be the means of wide-spread evil, instead of general good. And that this is, to a great extent, the present position of the Erie Canal, is universally admitted.

"To obviate these difficulties, enterprise has again undertaken to swell its dimensions to meet the enormous demands of *progress.* But in view of the vast regions which are common alike to it and the St. Lawrence, and which are as yet but in the infancy of their population and business, is it not probable, nay, is it not certain, judging by the past, that twenty years hence will find the Erie Canal again choked up with business—again *made little by progress?* When the magnificent tracts of country embraced in Michigan, Wisconsin, the northern portion of Ohio and Indiana, Illinois, Iowa, Minnesota, and the west and north-west portions of the State of New-York, which now wholly or largely use the Erie Canal as a highway to the ocean, come to be settled up, and to have, instead of some five or six millions of inhabitants, at least eighteen or twenty, what *mere canal,* with its hundred locks, and its hundred other impediments, will be equal to their vast business necessities? will be in keeping with their splendid progress? will satisfy their craving for rapidity, magnitude and commercial convenience? Will not the Erie Canal *then,* enlarged though it be, be but another added to the numerous examples, in America, *of progress utterly distancing enterprise, and prosperity shaming the calculations even of talent.*"

Are any further arguments necessary, after the above almost prophetic demand for an additional and enlarged avenue for Western trade, which cannot be surfeited by progress?

As a demand for improving and developing the mighty resources of these inland seas, the above arguments are not only unanswerable, but, on reflection, will be admitted to be incontrovertible.

Before concluding this Report, I would select this as the most fitting opportunity of thanking A. M. Ross, Esq., George Tait, and Walter Shanly, Esq., Civil Engineer, connected with the Grand Trunk Railway, for important statistical data and other information; Thomas Ridout and S. Fleming, Esqrs., Engineers of the Great Western and O. S. and H. Railways, for the use of plans; also to F. P. Rubidge, Esq., of the Board of Public Works, and Thomas Devine, Esq., of the Crown Lands Department, for the valuable information afforded by them, thereby facilitating my professional labors, and placing reliable data within reach, which could not otherwise be procured, without incurring further labor and loss of time, and entailing additional expense.

I have the honor to remain

Your obedient servant,

KIVAS TULLY.

Thomas Clarkson, Esq.,
President of the Board of Trade,
Toronto.

APPENDIX A.

" In regard to any prospective advantage for freight, I think you might mention the immense quantity of pine timber on the north shore of Lake Huron. Already large locations have been taken up, and extensive mills will be immediately erected. The description of mills about to be erected will make 30,000 feet per day, which, for each mill, will make 13,500 tons per annum, allowing one and a half tons per M., which is low. There will soon be about ten of these mills in operation, making annually 135,000 tons of freight, and with such encouragement as direct shipping to Liverpool, the West Indies, etc., the sawed pine of Lake Huron alone would employ 500,000 tons of shipping annually. Beside this freight of sawed lumber, there are the vast white oak tracts. It costs, at present, about $300 per thousand feet to take square white oak from the north of Lake Huron to Quebec, which is virtually a prohibition ; whereas, could it be shipped direct, one quarter of that sum would pay the extra transport, making an enhanced value for the timber on Lake Huron of two hundred per cent.

" With such a prospect, the amount of timber that would be manufactured can scarcely be calculated. But I should say that Canada alone, on Lake Huron, would require at least one thousand vessels, of one thousand tons each, to carry off her manufactures of sawed pine, square pine, both red and white ; pine masts and spars, square oak, staves, etc., etc. Besides, what a trade would immediately spring up in ship building. What better place could be selected for this purpose than the proposed outlet of the canal on Lake Huron (Nottawasaga river). At the mouth of the river is a deep reach of three and a half miles long, where one hundred or two hundred of the largest class of ships might be built at one and the same time, and, when built and afloat, they could be in perfect security.

" The timber for manufacturing them, both white oak, white and red pine timber, spars and masts, can be cut up the river, where there are some thousands of acres of these timbers, of the finest quality, which can be floated down to the ship yards with the greatest ease.

" Beside, this is only a small item in the prospect for freight. The great west is the country from which the bulk of freight must come. When we see what the making Lake Huron a part and parcel of the Atlantic is going to do, in the way of freight, what must we expect from Lake Michigan, and that great and almost unexplored inland sea, Lake Superior ?

" The impetus that the ship canal would give to the timber, mineral, fish and grain manufactories, would be incalculable. It would be the opening up to commerce of a new world, already teeming with life, and ready to manufacture to any amount, so long as there is a demand, as the supply of the above named articles, namely, timber, mineral, fish and grain, and of the best description, being practicably inexhaustible."

APPENDIX B.

THE TORONTO AND GEORGIAN BAY CANAL.

TORONTO, January 20th, 1858.

DEAR DOCTOR :

As the Report on the Toronto and Georgian Bay Ship Canal will soon be published, I would feel obliged by your stating any particulars with which you may be acquainted in reference to the same, for the purpose of publication, being assured that for several years you have taken an active interest in its promotion, as its original projector.

Believe me to remain, yours very truly,

KIVAS TULLY.

WM. REES, Esq., M.D., *Toronto.*

TORONTO, January 21, 1858.

DEAR SIR :

In reply to your note, desiring any particulars I may possess with reference to the Georgian Bay Canal, I have only to state, after having perused your valuable report, together with the opinion of Col. Mason, Con. E., one of the highest authorities in the United States, that anything I could communicate must be of very little value. I may, however, observe, that having made several explorations subsequent to calling public attention to the project through the columns of the *Courier*, in 1832, that I feel the more convinced of its practicability, whilst the rapid strides since made, both in Canada and the western States, has, I conceive, fully proved the justice of my numerous and very urgent appeals to government on that occasion, not merely with reference to the above, but also as to the claims of other important parts of the country to examination, in the direction of the Trent,* Ottawa, and Bay of Fundy, with views to perfecting the St. Lawrence navigation, from our vast inland seas to the Atlantic ; also, to affording greater encouragement to emigration and settlement, for it must be admitted that the fertile shores of Lake Huron, and the rich valleys of the Ottawa and St. Maurice, have been judiciously laid out at the

---

* On this suggestion of mine, Sir John Colborne did cause an examination of the chain of lakes between Lake Simcoe, the Trent and Rideau, connecting with the Ottawa, which resulted in the construction of certain locks, dams, and other partial improvements.

period referred to, our population, commerce and revenue, might have been nearly double what they are at present, and it cannot be denied that, on the settlement of the waste lands, the improvement of the St. Lawrence, together with the sea ports of Quebec and Montreal, mainly depend the future advancement and prosperity of this country.*

That our internal navigation will never be perfect, or commensurate with the requirements indicated by the progress of the last few years, and that it is merely a question of time (however absurd the idea may appear), when both the Georgian Bay and the Ottawa Canals shall be constructed, must be sooner or later acknowledged. By the former, vessels descending would have the advantage of the lake navigation, most prevailing winds and currents to tide water below Montreal, where they would arrive in the time at present occupied in reaching Buffalo. By the latter, or Ottawa canal, upward bound vessels would have the benefit of an inland, unobstructed, and more direct route to the head of the Georgian Bay, whilst in the lower St. Lawrence a further improvement may be effected, in the saving of from 500 to 600 miles, by means of a short canal at the head of the Bay of Fundy, thus throwing open the entire American and Colonial seaboard, and perhaps, at the same time, supplying the advantages contemplated by the proposed Champlain route, Chicago and other ports at the head of Lake Michigan and Lake Superior being thenceforth freed to the commercial world.

To the St. Lawrence, as the natural outlet of the great lakes and the regions west belongs the trade, is universally admitted; that with the advantage of being one-fourth the distance nearer Europe, together with the facilities presented for its improvement, the trade cannot longer continue to take the more southern channels, than until the above improvement shall have been effected, must be equally evident.†

Persevere then with the light heart and self reliance of a Canadian voyageur, who knows no obstacle; persevere in the great enterprise, and success is certain. The hope, the majesty of Canada is in her highways as the basis of her national wealth, as in her agriculture, her domestic industry and her commerce.

Bold, comprehensive and enlightened legislation, consonant with the spirit of the age, and in which the sister provinces‡ (whose union with the Canadas cannot long be protracted), should be invited to coöperate, is imperatively demanded.

---

* A Victoria, or extensive floating dock, has become as essential at Montreal as the Victoria Bridge, whilst the filling up and destruction of that noble harbor, once the pride of Quebec, should at once be prohibited, substituting as a ballast ground, through the medium of lighters, the river St. Charles, a simple means of facilitating, at the same time, the extension, north-easterly, of the limits (long a desideratum) to that important city.

† It having been ascertained that the finest and most approved quarries exist on certain islands in the vicinity or immediately on the line of the proposed canal, it may appear worthy of consideration how far, under such advantages, as in most parts of Europe, convict labor may not be employed.

‡ In connection with the above, the Halifax and St. Johns Inter-colonial Railway, both of which must sooner or later be constructed, deserve attention; and it would be well if the Governor of New Brunswick at once sought the possession of the land lying north of the St. Johns river, *by purchase*, which was so unjustly ceded by the Ashburton treaty, a small angular piece of territory of no great value or importance to the United States, but absolutely indispensable to the construction of a St. Johns and Quebec Railway. If properly represented to the United States government,

This vast and important appendage to the British Crown, possessed of the most promising destinies, in the enjoyment of every institution essential to intellectual and social developement, with one of the most practical forms of government that has ever existed, protected and fostered by the most widely extended and powerful empire the world has ever seen, should fill every heart with exultation and pride, and prove the most powerful incentive to energetic action, enterprise and emulation.*

I am truly yours,

WM. REES.

Kivas Tully, Esq.

Chief Eng'r Toronto & G. B. Canal,

Toronto.

---

considering the very great concessions made by Lord Ashburton, both in the settlement of the north-western boundary as well as in the settlement of the north-eastern boundary, no doubt but that it could be *purchased* at a fair valuation. Almost of equal importance to Canada, is that also comprised between the St. Louis and Red rivers at the head of Lake Superior.

* As indications of progress, the population of the North-west is already set down at 10,000,000, the city of Chicago 130,000. Cincinnati, in products, yielded in slaughtered cattle alone, during the last year, $8,000,000, and grain from all parts in proportion. Lake fisheries, 80 to 100,000 barrels. Whilst there are no less than three Pacific railways projected, showing that the great European highway is a prize worth contending for. $5,000,000, with as many acres of land and the labor of 5,000 convicts, would accomplish the work in five years. And it may be desirable at once to reserve for the benefit of such undertaking, that amount of the Crown lands throughout the line. Nor should any further time be lost by the government. Surveys and roads throughout the whole of that intersecting part of the country, should be made. Harbors and emigration depots should be provided, and thereby a more generally enlightened and liberal policy. Ought we not to be allowed an opportunity of redeeming ourselves from the stigma of a late Lieutenant-Governor, at that time somewhat merited, namely, that our population was not that of the parish of Mary le Bone, our revenue not that of an English Commoner, our boasted canals and harbors misplaced and but public patchwork, our enterprise and prosperity likened to a girdled tree; whilst the Westminster *Review* characterized the whole country as a workhouse. Thanks, however, to the establishment of a Provincial Board of Works, and perhaps to the circumstance of such a rebuke, our general progress and our national works so munificently endowed, will, at the present period, well compare with those of the most favored of other countries, whilst our great natural and commercial advantages prove superior to any on the whole of this continent. Then let our Provincial representatives be made sensible, that the greater interests of the country lie a little beyond their own doors or the mere frontier line of settlement, and the real and material source of wealth remains to be developed, and are to be mainly sought in opening up, settling the internal great thoroughfare indicated above, and which will be found as picturesque and fertile as the valleys of the Hudson and Mohawk, which it surpasses in the extent and magnitude of its water power. To succeed, however, in securing the confidence of capitalists, and attracting respectable emigrants to our views, the great moral interests must not be overlooked. Sectional jealousies and asperities, party feuds and party processions, are as inimical to the peace and prosperity of a new country as they are degrading to the whole community, and should, by an appeal to the good sense, pride and patriotism of the people, be by mutual consent forever extinguished. The more comprehensive designs of a union with our maritime provinces, the Inter-colonial Railway and Ocean Mail service, when received in connection with our accessions to the North-western territory, and the various American projected railway routes to the Pacific, cannot fail to favorably awaken the attention of the Imperial Government to what has long been foreshadowed, the establishing at no distant period of a regular Pacific portage; and it would be an enterprise worthy the Hudson's Bay Company, considering their deep interest and intimate knowledge of that highly interesting country, at once to plan out on the south branch of the noble Saskatchewan, the foundation of a *great central city* of the North-west, which would doubtless be followed by a great military or governmental high road.

APPENDIX C.

Meteorological Mean Results at the Toronto Observatory.

MONTH	Mean Barometer (Mean of 12 & 13 years.)	TEMPERATURE Mean (Mean of 17 years.)	TEMPERATURE Max. (July, Mean of 17 years.)	TEMPERATURE Min. (Feb'y, Mean of 17 years.)	TEMPERATURE Range (Mean of 17 years.)	NORMAL TEMP. Lat. 43°40' N. (Dove's Tables)	NORMAL TEMP. Therm. annu'ly (Mean of 17 years.)	RAIN Days (Mean of 17 years.)	RAIN Inches (Mean of 16 & 17 years.)	SNOW Days (Mean of 17 years.)	SNOW Inches (Mean of 14 years.)	Total moisture in inches (Mean of 17 years rain, 14 " snow.)	WIND Result'nt direct'n (Resultant of 9 years)	WIND Result'nt velocity (Resultant of 9 years)	WIND Mean velocity (Mean of 9 years)	WIND Mean force (Mean of 7 years.)
		deg. m.	deg. m.	deg. m.	deg. m.	deg. m	deg. m.	d. h.		d. h.			deg.	Miles.	Miles.	Lbs.
January	29.626	23.87	43.51	5.42	45.94	22.8	9.97	4.4	1.595	10.6	13.4	2.935	N. 72W.	2.78	7.45	0.70
February	29.625	23.65	43.72	5.18	49.50	34.7	12.65	3.4	1.020	10.8	17.7	2.190	N. 70W.	2.98	7.37	0.75
March	29.6314	29.93	51.69	4.22	47.66	40.1	10.16	5.3	1.512	8.1	10.3	2.342	N. 58W.	3.19	7.50	0.66
April	29.6061	41.88	65.62	19.94	45.12	50.2	6.61	9.9	2.537	2.5	1.9	2.474	N. 19W.	1.98	6.71	0.56
May	29.5635	51.46	74.44	31.24	43.35	64.6	6.65	10.5	3.082	0.5	0.1	3.079	N. 13W.	1.35	5.91	0.43
June	29.551	61.41	77.59	40.49	43.35	64.6	8.19	10.2	3.651			3.651	N. 8W.	0.51	4.41	0.29
July	29.5933	66.88	77.88	47.49	40.88	68.5	1.72	7.2	3.565			3.565	S. 5W.	0.31	4.53	0.29
August	29.6301	65.44	71.89	46.19	37.89	68.5	2.44	9.5	2.634			2.634	S. 57W.	0.89	5.29	0.19
September	29.6541	58.44	71.88	34.11	47.59	61.5	3.46	10.7	4.436	1.9	1.1	4.436	N. 49W.	0.90	5.29	0.36
October	29.6317	51.19	66.21	24.45	41.79	53.8	8.61	11.1	2.925	4.9	8.0	2.910	N. 68W.	1.35	6.42	0.85
November	29.612	36.79	52.71	15.58	39.12	43.2	6.40	9.2	2.923	14.4	11.4	2.523	N. 70W.	1.71	6.73	0.65
December	29.6463	26.02	44.60	1.29	45.89	36.0	9.5	5.1	1.589			2.979	N. 75W.	2.8	7.4	0.64
Mean, etc.	29.6190	41.15	77.8	5.38	44.51	51.0	6.8	96.2	30.759	51.1	61.9	36.910			6.12	0.50

DATA. *(Mean of 12 & 13 years, etc.)*

APPENDIX D.

GEOLOGICAL DESCRIPTION.

By reference to Sir William Logan's map, illustrating the physical structure of the Western District of Upper Canada, it will be observed that the proposed canal, commencing at the Humber Bay situated in the Hudson River group, crosses the line of division between this and the Utica slate about twenty-three miles from Lake Ontario, and the line of division of the Trenton limestone, thirty-three miles from Lake Ontario, comprising the "Ridges" in King. Route No. 1 continues in this group to the mouth of the Nottawasaga River.

The whole of the proposed routes pass through the lower silurian formation, except fifteen miles of the northern portion of route No. 2, which crosses the line of division between the lower silurian and Laurenbian series of the Geological survey.

Route No. 3 would also commence in the Hudson river group, crossing the lines of division of the Utica slate and Trenton groups, forty and fifty miles from Lake Ontario respectively, and continuing in the latter group to the mouth of the Nottawasaga River.

In Sir William Logan's paper on the physical structure of the Western District, etc., published in the August number [1854] of the Canadian Journal, the position which refers to this locality is as follows:

"Taking these rocks in the general groupings, it will be perceived by the map that the lower silurian series, by a change in the strike from west to north-west, sweeps round from Lake Ontario to the Georgian Bay, and proceeds thence by the north side of the Manitaulin Islands, and the north shore of Lake Huron to the northern peninsula of Michigan, gradually curving to Green Bay in Lake Michigan. The upper silurian follows them. The Niagara limestone at the base aids in forming the neck of land separating and holding up Lake Erie and Lake Ontario, and continues in a ridge along the Blue Mountains, and the promontory terminating at Cabots Head and Cape Hurd, of which promontory the chain of the Manitaulin Islands is only an interrupted prolongation."

The Hudson river group is exposed in front of the new garrison, west of Toronto, during the lowest lake level, and can be distinctly traced along the banks of the river Humber as far as Berwick, on the south side of the ridges, a distance of fourteen miles, indicating an inclination of about twenty feet to the mile in this direction; on the north side of the ridges no trace of this group has been discovered along the line of survey.

On Lot 24 in the 9th lon. of Albion township, a limestone crops out, which from good authority is stated to be a portion of the Trenton group; if this is the case the line of division between this group and the Utica slate should be drawn eight miles farther west than is indicated on the geological map, and the whole of the deep excavation in the township of King would be in the Trenton group.

As the Trenton limestone, where it crops out on the river St. Lawrence, is proved to be very suitable for building purposes, the locks on the St. Lawrence canals having been constructed with this material, the work on the excavation will be considerably lessened in quantity, and as the limestone can be used in the construction of the locks, a considerable saving in the cost would be effected.

In connection with this question, the following description of the subsidence of "drift" period in Sir Charles Lyell's Manuel of Geology, page 135, will be interesting to the advocates of this important undertaking.

From the distinct evidence of drift on the surface of the ridges, corresponding with Sir Charles Lyell's description, there can be no doubt but that the upper portion of the deep excavation will be through the "drift" described on the Trenton group, thereby reducing the *inseperable* difficulties to those of time and money.

" By the hypothesis of such a slow and gradual subsidence of the land, we may account for the fact that almost everywhere in North America and Northern Europe, the boulder formation rests in a polished and furrowed surface of rock, a fact by no means obliging us to imagine, as some think, that the polishing and grooving action was, as a whole, anterior in date to the transportation of the erratics.

" During the successive depression of the highland, varying originally in height from 1000 to 3000 feet above the sea level, every portion of the surface would be brought down by turns to the level of the ocean, so as to be converted first into a coast line and then into a shoal; and at length, after being well scored by the stranding upon it of thousands of icebergs, might be sunk to a depth of several hundred fathoms.

" By the constant depression of land the coast would recede further and further from the successively formed zones of polished and striated rock, each outer zone becoming in its turn so deep under water as to be no longer grated upon by the heaviest icebergs. Such sunken areas would then simply serve as receptacles of mud, sand and boulders, dropped from melting ice, perhaps to a depth, scarcely, if at all inhabited by urtacea and zoophytes; meanwhile, during the formation of the unstratified and unfossiliferous mass in deeper water, the smoothing and furrowing of shoals and breaches is still going on elsewhere, upon and near the coast in full activity.

" If at length the subsidence should cease, and the direction of the movement of the earth's crust be reversed, the sunken area covered with drift would be slowly reconverted into land.

" The boulder deposit, before emerging, would then for a time be brought within the action of the waves, tides and currents, so that its upper portion being partially disturbed, would have its materials rearranged and stratified. Streams also flowing from the land would in some places throw down layers of sediment upon the till. In that case, the order of superposition will be first and uppermost, sand, loam and gravel occasionally fossiliferous. Secondly, an unstratified and unfossiliferous mass, for the most part of much older date than the preceding, with angular erratics or with boulders interspersed; and, Thirdly, beneath the whole, a surface of polished and furrowed rock."

APPENDIX E.

Magnitude of the Lakes, from Disturnell's Trip Through the Lakes.

NAME.	Area.	Length, in miles.	Greatest Breadth	Average Breadth	Coast Line.	Depth, in feet.	Elevation above the Sea.	REMARKS.
Superior	52,800	420	160	80	1050	1000	600	The Sault Ste Marie Canal connects Lakes Superior and Huron. Size of the locks, 350 feet long, 70 feet wide, 10 feet lift. Canal one mile in length.
Huron	22,500	260	110	70	705	960	574	
Michigan	21,260	230	82	58	655	900	578	
Erie	11,800	250	60	38	570	204	564	Welland canal connects Lakes Erie and Ontario; 28 miles in length.
Ontario	8,200	180	58	40	410	600	234	High water, 5 feet above lowest level.
Georgian Bay	6,000	140	55	40	310	500	574	" " 4 " "
Simcoe	561	35	18	10	108	120	704	" " 2 " "
St. Clair	332	20	25	15	60	8 to 20	568	Annual loss at the Flats, $1,000,000, besides detention six days each trip.
Champlain	1,130	120	12	10	260	54 to 282	90	Chambly and Champlain canals connect the
Green Bay	1,900	100	25	18	220	100	475	St. Lawrence and Hudson. Twelve miles and 66 miles long, respectively.
Nippissing	560	40	18	12	120	unknown	643	

NOTE.—From Anticosti Island to Fond du Lac, Lake Superior............ 2,806 miles.

Coast line of the River St. Lawrence and Lakes............ 5,657 "

Navigable tributaries of the St. Lawrence............ 500 "